ES

L

HW M.P.

Iron Claw's Revenge

Other Avalon Books by Terrell L. Bowers

BLACK CLOUD OVER GUNSTOCK
RAILROAD WAR!
LASSITO'S LAST WAR
DESTINY'S TRAIL
TRAIL TO JUSTICE
CHEYENNE BROTHERS
FIGHTING LUCANES
THE DEVIL'S ROPE
VENDETTA!
SKULL MOUNTAIN BANDIT
THE MASKED COWPOKE
SINCLAIR'S DOUBLE WAR

IRON CLAW'S REVENGE

TERRELL L. BOWERS

AVALON BOOKS
THOMAS BOUREGY AND COMPANY, INC.
401 LAFAYETTE STREET
NEW YORK, NEW YORK 10003

PRINTED IN THE UNITED STATES OF AMERICA
BY HADDON CRAFTSMEN, SCRANTON, PENNSYLVANIA

Iron Claw's Revenge

Chapter One

The air smelled of death. Combined with the hum of scavenger flies and the circling of a pair of vultures, it was a sure indication that something—or someone—had departed this world.

Though as tired and thirsty as his rider, Kit Montgomery's horse shied away from the nearby creek. Most animals steered clear of death whenever possible. Kit nudged him on with a touch of his heels. The water was hidden by a wide chaparral. The brush was too tangled and dense to ride through, so Kit took the longer way, skirting the worst of the brush. He didn't have to ride very far before he discovered the source of the stench.

There were six of them—Owatawna Indians—scattered about in grotesque positions. They had been scalped and mutilated. Kit stepped down from his horse and visited each body. Two were only children, two were young women, and two were very elderly, apparently a married couple. They'd had a camp next to the stream. The remains of some dried fish and cactus pods were mute testimony that they'd been gathering stores for the coming winter.

Kit fought back his nausea. The family had been dead at least eight or ten hours. Only the fact that two Indian ponies were moving about had kept the buzzards from swooping down to pick the family's bones.

There was nothing to do for any of the victims, who had all been shot at least once and then scalped. Only the old man appeared to have put up a struggle. He'd crawled a few feet and died.

Filled with bitter hatred, Kit checked around for sign, and then buried the entire group in a shallow grave. When the task was finished, he stuck a branch into the mound and draped it with the victims' beads and necklace pieces. If the family's friends came looking, they could deduce the fate of their loved ones.

He stood with his hat in his hand and looked skyward. "God, I reckon You and the Great Spirit are One and the same, and that anyone who believes in a Supreme Being is one of Your children. That being the case, I commit these six souls to Your safekeeping. Amen."

The sky was growing dark, but Kit had to get to Fort Ryan and tell the soldiers what he'd found, so they could warn and protect the settlers and any travelers. Chief Iron Claw was not known for overlooking crimes against Indians. Once he learned of the deaths of his people, he would demand revenge.

Kit knew the trails, even in the dark. He'd joined the Army just as the War Between the States was ending. In the years that followed, he scouted for Brevet Brigadier General Henry Carrington in Nebraska during a westward march to Julesburg, Colorado, later moving with the troops to Fort Bridger in the southwest corner of Wyoming and then to Camp Douglas at Salt Lake City. He'd grown tired of endless campaigns and fighting. When a mediator was needed at Fort Ryan to deal for some hostages, Kit had volunteered. Somehow the job had lasted three years.

He rode through the pines quietly. His horse, Dusky, was a light-stepping animal that seldom stepped on dry sticks or noisily rubbed against the brush. Dusky would stand still for an hour at a time, and he had never shied from gunfire. A skeptic would call that good training, but Kit knew that the coal-black gelding was simply smart.

It took several hours of hard riding to reach

the fort. Knowing the captain would be in bed by then, Kit saw to his horse and went to the tavern to get a meal.

As luck would have it, the tavern was filled with the Saturday-night crowd, which included a dozen troopers, a couple of past-their-prime ladies, and a few settlers from nearby farms and ranches. As Kit took a table in a dark corner, he caught sight of several trappers. He hadn't met them, but he knew them on sight.

Al Squash was drunk. The noise he made while drinking was almost as irritating as his smell. He wore a cutoff buffalo robe, a floppy straw hat, and boots that reached his knees. A barrel-chested man, he had a scar on one cheek, a month's growth of beard on his face, and the yellow teeth of a man who chewed and smoked tobacco to excess. Kit usually ignored the big blowhard, but Al got his attention when he produced a sack of scalps—Indian scalps.

"These six Owatawna ain't gonna give us no more trouble!" Al guffawed loudly. "Me and the boys caught them near Little Bear country—and we turned the dirty beggars into six *good* Indians!"

Though his announcement was met with a few shouts and cheers from the cattlemen and farmers, the soldiers present weren't so enthusiastic. They had better sense than to cheer a massacre. Some of them even exchanged knowing looks of dread.

"Didn't you blue-bellies hear me?" Al challenged the soldiers. "We saved you from hunting down six of those red devils!"

Kit rose from his table. He hadn't gotten his supper yet, he'd ridden twenty miles in the dark, and he'd buried those very six Indians. Feeling a bit surly, he crossed the room and planted himself in front of Al. Even as the big trapper eyed him suspiciously, Kit appraised the handful of scalps. "You must be some pretty tough customers, Squash. Only the four of you against six Owatawna."

"We took them by surprise," the trapper replied smugly. "They had no idea what hit them."

Kit held up one of the scalps. He showed it to the men in the room, allowing all of them a good look.

"This young squaw probably put up quite a fight. I figure she was at least twelve years old," he said bitingly. "About the same age as the boy."

Al sputtered, his grin lost instantly. He reached for the scalps, but Kit turned away deftly. He pulled out a second scalp, full of gray and white streaks. "And this old man—

bet you had your hands full with him too. Takes a pretty brave man to tackle someone twice his own age."

"Gimme those!" Al grabbed for the bag of scalps, his flushed face twisted into an ugly sneer. Kit let him take the bag, but he turned to face the ranchers and settlers, who were no longer cheering. Killing children—even Indian children—was nothing to brag about.

"Iron Claw won't stand for this. He'll be out for blood." Kit's voice was full of conviction. "If I had a family, I'd surely get home and look after them. This drunken scum has likely started a war."

Al took hold of Kit's shoulder and jerked him around. "Now, you hold on, Montgomery! We all know that you're an Indian lover, but it ain't so for the rest of us. We've got to kill those redskins any way we can. If we don't kill them, they'll kill us!"

"And if we kill them all, we can trap their game and take their land. Once we get rid of them, the West will be a safer place." Kit's sarcasm was obvious. "Only one thing is wrong with that, Squash—they were here first!"

"Didn't I tell you that he was an Indian lover?" Al said loudly. "Listen to him, and your wives and children will end up being scalped."

"Indians didn't invent scalping, Squash. It got started when the British and the French began paying for scalps over a hundred years ago!"

Al didn't like the way the debate was going. Being the bigger man, he decided simply to shut Kit up with one swipe of his huge fist. But Kit ducked the mighty blow, countering with a bone-crushing right of his own that sent Al reeling against the bar. Before he could recover, Kit punished him with brutal rights and lefts, driving him down to the floor. Al could only cower against the hail of blows. Though strong hands caught Kit by the shoulder and tried to drag him off, he continued to pound at the man's face with his rock-hard knuckles.

"That's enough!" A familiar voice finally cut through the red haze of his fury. "He's had enough, Montgomery!"

Kit allowed himself to be pulled off the beaten trapper. Breathing hard, he shrugged loose at once, but didn't try to attack again.

"Killing him won't do any good," Sergeant Roaker was saying.

A bald man blocked Kit's path. It was Al's friend Kelly, who had probably helped him kill the Indians. "Al won't take this lying down," Kelly told Kit.

Kit looked at the dazed trapper. "Seems to me that's exactly how he's taking it."

The sergeant led Kit outside. The night air was crisp and fresh, a big improvement over the smoke-filled tavern. The two men began walking to the fort together.

"Got to hand it to you, Montgomery. Those four men are about the worst in the territory. Al, Kelly, Mole, or Curray—any one of them would be happy to put a bullet in your back."

"I didn't go looking for a fight. You saw those scalps. They belonged to a family, Roaker. I buried them this afternoon. Not a brave among them, either."

"That means reprisals," the sergeant observed, adding, "and I know something else that's going to round out your day."

"What's that?"

Roaker let out a long sigh. "I'll let the captain tell you tomorrow morning. I've heard only rumors."

"What kind of rumors?"

They stopped in the middle of the trail. Roaker lowered his head, his shoulders bowed. He appeared very tired. "No more buying back hostages," he told Kit.

Kit heard the words, but they didn't sink in. "Not buy hostages?"

"That's all I've heard. You can speak to

Captain Yount about it in the morning. If you haven't eaten, I've got some hardtack and a tin of peaches at the barracks."

Kit could only nod. He couldn't believe what he'd heard. If the Army quit paying for hostages, what would happen to people who were captured?

Chapter Two

Kit waited until after reveille and breakfast call to enter Captain Yount's headquarters. Roaker was already there. He nodded toward the closed door of Yount's office.

"He's waiting for you, Montgomery. The news ain't good."

The commander of the fort looked up as Kit walked into the room.

"Close the door, Montgomery. You want a cup of coffee?"

Kit shook his head, standing in front of the man's large oak desk. The fact that Yount wouldn't look him in the eye meant Roaker had heard right: The government would no longer pay ransom for hostages.

"It's been taken out of my hands," the captain apologized at once. "You know I'm not the kind of man to beat around the bush."

"Yes, sir."

10

"Roaker told me about the scalps and the trouble last night. The three of us know that Iron Claw is sure to seek revenge. That massacre was exactly the type of excuse his brother has been looking for to start an all-out war."

Kit agreed. "Puma will want to kill every white in the country. Iron Claw has been holding him back, but now. . . ."

He didn't have to finish. Yount leaned back in his wooden chair and folded his arms, looking much older than his forty years.

"I'm going to need scouts, Montgomery."

"No thanks, Captain. I've spent a lot of time winning the trust of those Indians. I've bargained with Iron Claw a dozen times. I wouldn't want to be out in the hills tracking him down."

"No one can stop the westward expansion," Captain Yount declared. "The Indians must accept that."

"It won't happen, Captain. No one can tame the wind."

Yount drummed his fingers on the top of his desk. "I know that you've been a man of peace these last three years, Montgomery, and that you've made some friends among the Indians. But this new policy comes right from the top. The Department of War has ordered us to withdraw all offers of money for the release of hostages taken by Indians."

"I hope the hostages agree with the War Department, sir."

Yount slammed his fist down on the desk and stood up. "Blast it all, Montgomery! I don't like this any more than you. But we've been paying ransom for three years! Some Indians have been making their living by raiding wagon trains or farms and stealing women and children for ransom. We've got to put a stop to it."

Kit leaned over the desk and looked hard at the captain. "And what will happen to those hostages now? What if the Indians decide to kill them rather than take them prisoner?"

"If they do, we'll come down hard on them. There are more troops being dispatched from Kansas City. Within a week, we'll have a second company to garrison the fort. If the Owatawna decide to declare war, we'll be ready."

Kit laughed humorlessly. "No one is ever ready for an Indian attack, Captain. If war breaks out, a river of blood will be spilled from here to New Mexico and Utah. I know you remember the Battle of Sand Creek, where a dozen Colorado Volunteers died, along with over two hundred braves, women, and children. Those were mostly Cheyenne and Arapaho. These are Owatawna. The Cheyenne fought solo, without any leadership. The Arapaho fought in small bands, with little or no organization. But the Owatawna have leaders and will follow a chain of command. They can mount raids that will pick your two companies apart. The Army won't be fighting a few small chaotic bands of warriors; they'll oppose a nation of fighting men."

"I wish I could change the situation, Montgomery, but I'm only an officer following orders. I'd like you to sign on and help."

Kit shook his head. "I've been too close to them, Captain. I've shared their meals, their lodging, and their pipes at night by the fire. They don't all trust me, but I've walked among them."

"I can understand how you feel," Captain Yount said.

"I'm resigning my post, as you no longer have need of a mediator."

The captain stuck out his hand. "I wish you luck, Montgomery. If you change your mind, there is always a job open."

Kit shook hands with the captain and turned to go.

"Keep an eye on your back trail," Yount

warned. "Those trappers will be after your hide. That Al Squash is a mean cuss."

"I'll be a little harder to take than one of their beaver pelts or those six Owatawna they murdered."

"So long, Montgomery."

Kit went out, said good-bye to Roaker, and then rounded up his horse. He felt the need to get away, to put miles between himself and the fort. War was imminent, he felt certain of that. He had a mind to ride away and not look back—except to watch out for Al Squash and his friends.

The day was a duplicate of many before it, the stagnant air unmoving, the boiling dust churned into clouds by the oxen and the wheels of the six Conestoga wagons. The last wagon in the small train had to endure the worst conditions, being enveloped by the sand and billowing dirt of the first five wagons.

Deana Shaw detested the powdery substance that kept getting in her eyes and that coated her hair and skin. Her clothes were white from the swirling dust. She tugged her bonnet forward on her head, shading her face from the relentless sun. She mopped her brow and throat with her handkerchief, leaving it smudged and dirty. Breathing was difficult, as the stifling dust burned her sinuses.

Squinting into the nebulous cloud of whirling dust, Deana attempted to see the distant range of mountains. It would be cooler there, where grass would replace the thick, dirty cloud that engulfed them. How she relished the thought of the fresh, flower-scented woods and the springs of clear, sweet water. Traveling through the mountains would be more laborious, but she would welcome the change.

"Are you ready to get back up on the wagon, Deana?" her father called down from the seat of the rolling wagon at her side.

"I'll walk a little longer," she replied, only to get a mouthful of sand and grit.

"Getting mighty hot," he called down again. "Don't you get overheated."

She tried to smile at him, but the effort was too great. Her spirit had been drained by the endless days of marching, camping, cooking over open fires, and suffering under the torrid sun while crossing a vast wasteland of cactus and sagebrush. The promised land still loomed in another part of the country, miles and miles away.

Deana sidestepped a yucca plant and thought over her decision to join her father in seeking their fortune in the territory. For as long as she could remember, it had been his dream to carve out a home in the wilderness and live off the land. He had often spoken about making his own destiny and determining his own future. Her mother's death had provided the impetus to pursue his dreams. They had packed up and joined several other families, all heading westward to begin new lives.

She had a number of misgivings about her decision. It was frightening to think of not seeing another settlement for weeks at a time, while totally dependent on what nature supplied.

And there had been other alternatives available. She'd been pursued by more than one man in their town. She could have selected a husband and remained there. But none of her suitors had stirred her soul. She secretly yearned for an adventurous, dashing hero. She wanted a real man, someone who would always think of her first and would want to change the world to suit her. He would be romantic and caring, able to share her intimate thoughts. He would be young at heart, but mature in his decisions, protective of her and their children. And he would always enjoy holding her close and whispering sweet words in her ear.

Peering off into the distance once more, she realized that she was smiling dreamily. Sobering, she thought how wonderful a bath would feel. She dabbed at her forehead with the handkerchief once more. Oh, for a cool, refreshing drink from a mountain stream! If only she. . . .

A bansheelike cry split the arid afternoon air. It was followed instantly by shrieks and a yell of warning. Gunshots sounded as one of the wagons bolted away.

Deana stifled her own scream, putting a hand over her mouth. She turned toward her father, her heart suddenly thundering in her chest. He was pulling his rifle out from under the wagon seat. He shouted at her to get into the wagon, but one of the team dropped to its knees and rolled onto its side. Even as the horse kicked and writhed in death, her father jumped down.

Deana started toward him, but a painted horse and rider flashed up in front of her. The lathered beast slammed against her, knocking her to the ground. She barely glimpsed the back of a half-naked, brown-skinned warrior, his plaited hair bouncing in the wind.

She crawled on her hands and knees, frantic to get to the safety of their wagon. Her father fired his gun again and again as she squirmed under the wagon and slid in next to him.

The dust was churned by a dozen horses racing past. Deana put her hands over her ears to shut out the Indians' terrible war cries, which were intermingled with wails of anguish and fear from those in the wagon train. The mighty roar of gunfire echoed up the distant mountain walls as the small band of travelers made a desperate stand.

Indians streaked in front of them but provided no targets. The warriors used their horses like shields, hanging over the side and shooting right under the animal's neck or belly. The air was filled with gunfire, shrieks of terror, and mournful laments of death.

Deana screamed as a bullet kicked dirt up into her face. She heard her father moan, and she blinked away the sand to see a crimson blotch appear on his shirtfront.

"Father!" she cried, trying to rise and help him. She stopped abruptly, for he had aimed his rifle at her!

"Forgive me, my darling daughter," he pleaded over the noise and confusion.

Deana's eyes were transfixed by the weapon—aimed right at her head. She opened her mouth to speak, but he pulled the trigger—

Deana flinched at the resounding click. The gun was empty. Frozen in terror, she was unable to think or react as her father fumbled with a bullet, trying to get it into the chamber.

His breathing was ragged, his face ashen and twisted in pain.

A man ran past the wagon. He had no gun. He was waving his arms frantically, screaming at the top of his lungs. Through her tear-blurred vision, Deana saw an Indian on horseback race after him, carrying a short lance. The screaming ceased suddenly, and the man disappeared into the swirling dust.

Deana knew she had to get away, to escape or hide. But she couldn't leave her father. He had the gun loaded, working the bullet into the chamber. She shut her eyes, awaiting the bullet that would save her from the hands of the Indians. With tears streaming down her cheeks, she held her breath. . . .

A blast shattered the air.

Deana sucked in her breath, knowing the impact of the bullet would be painlessly swift and deadly. But there was no impact, no end to the screams and gunfire. She opened her eyes slowly, incredulous that she was still alive.

Her father lay on his face, the rifle still clutched in his lifeless hands. The shot hadn't come from his gun. Swept up by an overwhelming panic, she looked up from under the wagon—right into the painted face of an Indian.

Unable to suppress her terror, she screamed,

cringing away from the sweat-stained, sneering man. Wearing only a loincloth and a warbonnet, his black hair in plaits, he laughed at her. All Deana could see was the man's frightening face, his eyes shining like black buttons, a wicked sneer on his lips, as he dropped to his knees, poking at her with his rifle.

She clawed at her father's gun, trying to jerk it out from under his body. The Indian was too quick for her, ripping the rifle out of her hands. With a cruel, contemptuous smile, he tossed the gun out of her reach.

Deana scrambled away, trying to crawl out from under the wagon to the opposite side. A powerful hand clamped around her ankle and pulled her onto her stomach. She cried out in fear, digging into the hot sand with her fingers, as the Indian dragged her out into the open. She would have fought against him, but he used his own weapon as a club upon her. The force of being hit blackened her world, and she could taste the dust in her mouth, but there was no pain, no other sensation. Her fleeting last thought was that she was being killed and the absence of pain was a gift from the Almighty.

Chapter Three

It was early afternoon when Kit finally spotted the moving specks far down on his back trail. He had to glimpse them only once to know they were following him. Al Squash and his buddies were on their way to even the score with him. At four to one, the odds were heavily in their favor.

As he rode, Kit contemplated what moves he should make, considering whether to lose the trappers or to set them afoot. He rode along for a while, until the sound of buzzing brought him and his horse to a halt. When he noted the source of the noise, he smiled mischievously. Here was the solution to his problem.

The trail narrowed through the trees, some with branches so low that a man had to ride around them or lie low in the saddle to get under them. At one such point on the trail, it was easier to push aside a protruding limb than

21

to duck under it. That particular tree was also neatly situated between two outcrops of boulders, so it was ideal for what Kit had in mind.

Slowly and carefully, he used two long sticks to relocate a giant hornets' nest. He meticulously nestled the oblong hive up in the tree limbs. Finally it was secure—but only until the branch was moved. A strong wind or someone moving the limb would certainly dislodge it.

With a chuckle of anticipation, Kit carefully brushed out all trace of tracks on the ground. When he'd finished, he rode his horse directly up to the tree and ducked low under the branch. A hundred yards up the trail, he hid behind the brush to see if his plan would work.

Al was leading the way, watching with his good eye. His left eye was swollen shut from one of Kit's well-placed blows—a constant reminder of the humiliation he'd suffered in the tavern.

"He's slowed his pace some, Al," Kelly observed. "You think he knows we're after him?"

"That don't make a lot of sense, Kelly," Curray argued. "If he knowed we were back here, he'd step up his horse, not slow him down."

"Could be that he figures he's safe," Mole declared. "He might think we'd not follow him this far."

"You guys pipe down!" Al snapped over his shoulder. "Voices carry a long way in these hills. We'll sure enough catch that hombre when he stops for the night."

Kelly laughed. "You sound a might touchy, Al. I think Montgomery got your goat."

"I wasn't ready for him. He hit me before I knew what was going on."

"I seem to remember you took the first swing."

Al glowered at Kelly. "I was only going to shut him up. By the time I found out I was in a fight, he had me pinned to the floor. I'll give Montgomery credit, he has one heck of a punch."

"He's almost as big as you," Kelly noted. "I don't think I'd like tangling with him either."

"What are we gonna do to him?" Curray asked.

Al thought about that for a moment. "Exactly what we did to those six red devils. Since Montgomery is such an Indian lover, I figure he'd enjoy the same kind of death."

They were all still laughing at that as Al shoved a low-hanging branch out of his path. Something slipped through the upper branches and slammed onto the ground.

"Hey!" Kelly cried, swatting at the sudden swarm of hornets.

"Yeow!" Mole yelled. He yanked his horse around toward the nearest opening in the rocks. "Hornets' nest!" he shouted.

"Help!" Curray howled, batting at an angry wasp. "They're everywhere!"

From up the hill, Kit watched the horses bolting in all directions, crashing through the brush to get away from the mad hornets. The riders were hanging on for dear life and swatting at the stinging insects.

Turning his horse up the trail, Kit began moving again. "Mess with a bee—you're going to get stung," he said philosophically.

When he reached a small brook, he directed his horse into it and turned back the way he'd come. He followed the stream until he reached a rocky bank, then left the creek and kept to the hard ground. After a quarter of a mile, he resumed his original direction.

The terrain was mountainous for many miles before leveling out into the vast plains, a desertlike basin that stretched as far as the eye could see. He needed to skirt the desert far enough to cross it without being seen. He knew where there were a number of arroyos and washes farther to the south. He would ride across the open ground by sticking to the low gullies and washes. If he could lose the trappers, he'd only have to worry about the

Owatawna. Even Al Squash should avoid their part of the country.

He topped the zenith of a hillock and looked out over the open expanse of desert, staring at a distant column of smoke. With his field glass, he was able to see a group of wagons. Though too far away to make out many details, he could tell the smoke was not from any fire for cooking. The wagons themselves were burning.

Kit let out a deep, sorrowful sigh. The Owatawna had not waited long to seek revenge. Feeling both regret and apprehension, he directed his horse toward the wagon train. He would do what he could—even if all he could do was bury the dead.

Al stood on the ledge, scrutinizing the hills and trees below. He rubbed the swellings on his arms and ears. Kit Montgomery had had his last laugh. No matter how long it took, Al would hunt down that Indian lover and kill him.

"See anything?" Kelly came out to stand next to him.

"Some smoke over that way. It appears to be in the open country toward the plains."

Kelly looked in that direction. "Wouldn't be a campfire, not this early."

"My guess is some travelers met up with some Owatawna."

Kelly let out a sigh. "Killing that family stirred them up like those hornets Montgomery left for us. I told you that it was a mistake to kill them."

Al looked hard at him. "You ain't going soft on me, are you, Kelly?"

"You know better than that," the other replied. "But killing that family was bound to cause trouble."

"Trouble is what I intend for Montgomery. He set us up good."

"I was keeping an eye out for almost any kind of trick," Kelly said ruefully, "but I never expected a hornets' nest."

"And now we've lost his trail," Al complained.

But Kelly nodded toward the dark column of smoke. "If that smoke is from the Owatawna, Montgomery will be heading that way to see if he can help those travelers."

"Then that's where we're going too. I want him," Al said tightly.

"We ought to head up to Little Bear country again. Montgomery has warned us off. I think maybe we should. . . ."

"What's the matter with you, Kelly?" Al

spun on him. "I told you that I wanted that man!"

"At what price, Al? I think we should forget Kit Montgomery. He's the kind of man who can set a trap and kill one of us every mile."

"I've heard the stories, Kelly. I've heard them till I'm sick to death."

"Some of those tales are true. He's good with a knife and a handgun, and he can hit a target from half a mile away with his Sharps buffalo rifle."

"He ain't got the killer instinct anymore, Kelly. He left the post so he wouldn't have to kill any of them redskins. He's lost his nerve."

"Maybe so, but we're on the edge of Iron Claw's hunting ground. That group of Indians you men killed belonged to his tribe. He and his brother are going to be scalp hunting. I don't like the idea of tangling with them."

"Kelly's right," Mole declared. "Montgomery ain't worth getting killed for. Why don't we forget about him?"

"We'll get him, Mole, and we'll get him tonight. If you've a mind to turn tail and run, you can pull out. I'm going to get that man, even if it's the last thing I do."

Covered with numerous welts from the hornet stings, the men didn't look much like four tough trappers—more like four beaten saddle tramps. But Al wanted his revenge. Since he was their leader, they would stick with him.

Chapter Four

Streaks of white-hot pain flashed through Deana's skull, like slivers of fire driven by massive hammers. Her head was being rocked back and forth by jarring, open-palmed slaps. The stinging blows finally made her fully conscious, and she tried to block them with her hands.

"Up, she-dog!" a deep voice hissed.

Deana blinked through the tears that flooded her eyes. She tried to obey, but her legs seemed like dead weights. Before she could manage to stand, she was slapped again.

"Wait!" she cried. "I need a little time!"

"Up, she-dog!" the Indian ordered her again.

Deana managed to get up, but she felt weak and dizzy. She felt the swollen bruise on the side of her head, which was throbbing with pain.

The Indian was the one who'd killed her father. Apparently he'd dragged her to his horse and taken her into the hills. Only a distant column of grayish smoke against the blue sky showed how far they were from the wagons.

Even as she tried to keep from fainting, the Indian tied her hands behind her with a short strip of rawhide. Then he slipped a noose over her head and tightened it about her neck.

"You fall, you die," he sneered, his face only inches from her own.

Deana wondered if everyone else had been killed. She and the Indian were the only people in sight. He mounted his horse and started toward the nearby hills. She walked along quickly, so the noose wouldn't tighten about her throat and strangle her.

Trudging after him, she had time to study the Indian. He rode the horse as if he were part of the animal. The horse was colorful, with black, white, and brown patches, four white stockings, and a black mane and tail. Its wooden saddle, covered with animal hide, showed her she'd been wrong in supposing that all Indians rode bareback.

The man draped his brightly colored war-bonnet on the pommel of the saddle, evidently to ease his discomfort from the heat. She had thought that he had only two braids, but a third, laced with beads and small ornaments, hung down his back. Proud and erect in the saddle, he seemed both haughty and arrogant.

The ache in her head became a steady pounding, but Deana soon had other miseries to think about. She hadn't taken a drink of water before the attack, and she'd swallowed a lot of dust. Her mouth was dry and sore. Her cheeks and the inside of her mouth were tender from being slapped. Forced to walk at a brisk pace, her throat coated inside with alkali and dust, she soon found it impossible to swallow. Her legs were fairly strong from the daily amount of walking she was used to, but moving faster and going uphill soon proved exhausting.

Dusk brought cooler air that might have been comfortable, but Deana was unable to think of anything but her growing thirst and the burning sensation in her lungs. A chipmunk chattered in the distance, and a bird fluttered ahead of them from bush to bush. Otherwise, the only sounds came from the horse's hooves and her own feet digging into the soft dirt.

The terrain had changed dramatically, for the sage and desert cactus were mostly gone. Columbines, yarrow, and low-mountain junipers and cedars appeared. In the distance, she could perceive firs and pines. The sand yielded to shale rock and mountain soil.

Hour after hour they continued the trek. Deana found it increasingly difficult to go on. With her arms tied behind her, it was hard to climb and maintain her balance. As the ground became more choppy and broken, she labored to keep up.

Her heavy skirt had been torn and was full of stickers and thorns. The cotton waist blouse was damp with perspiration, and her bonnet was too far back on her head to shade her face. Trying to climb a steep escarpment was too much for her. She dug her toes into the rocky soil, but her knees gave way.

"Wait!" she cried, falling forward.

Her cry didn't stop the Indian. He let the horse pull against the rope, and its slack tightened at once, strangling Deana. She was dragged a few feet before the Indian stopped.

Deana couldn't breathe, for the noose was secure about her throat, choking off her air passage. She squirmed forward, but couldn't draw a breath. Twisting her neck violently, she tried without success to loosen the rope.

"White woman has no night feet," the Indian declared, coming back to stand over her.

Just as she thought that she would pass out, he finally hooked his fingers between her throat and the rope and jerked the cord loose. She coughed and gagged as he removed the noose.

"Get up, she-dog. Many miles yet."

Gasping for air, Deana was carried away with helpless frustration, misery, sorrow, and rage. She glared up at the Indian. "You murdering savage! I'm not an animal to be—"

Something whistled in the dark. The end of the rope struck Deana on the forehead. She fell silent at once as the smarting blow burned a streak along her brow. She didn't cry out, but tears came into her eyes.

"White women all the same," the man said. "Like small children. Iron Claw know how treat women."

Deana kept her eyes lowered. "I'm very thirsty, Iron Claw. May I have a drink?"

"Water not far."

She risked an upward glance. The Indian was looking back over the trail they had followed.

"You speak English well," she observed, trying a new approach. "Where did you learn the white man's language?"

"Iron Claw was prisoner of white man. I learn much."

"Why did you attack us? We meant you no harm."

"White men kill my people. I kill white man's people. I think we will have war."

"W-what do you want with me?"

He looked down at her, a mixture of hate and rage in his eyes. She wondered if he was going to kill her right there and then.

"White women have use. If you good, you live. If you bad, you die. Get up, she-dog. We go to water."

That was enough to give her legs some strength. She got to her feet and staggered forward. Iron Claw mounted his horse and followed. Whenever she slowed down, he would prod her with a short lance. That always renewed her energy.

It was dusk by the time Kit reached the wagon train. He approached with his gun in hand, but the fighting had long since ceased. Nothing was left but the charred remains of several wagons—and the mutilated corpses of the travelers. The Owatawna had exacted a swift, terrible revenge.

Despite the stench of burning flesh and dried blood, Kit took time to look over the victims. There were sixteen in all, men, women, and several children. He spent a few minutes searching through belongings and reading sign. By sorting through the bits of clothing that the Indians had strewn about, he tried to account for all of the bodies. The new policy decreed that no bounty be paid for hostages, but the Owatawna might not know it yet. They might have taken. . . .

Kit paused near the last wagon. An elderly man lay beneath it. The fire had burned itself out, leaving much of the wagon bed intact. Clothes and a few items were left inside the wagon. Apparently the Indians had been in a hurry to leave, for many trinkets and garments had been left behind.

Inside the wagon, Kit found some things that belonged to a woman—one more than he had accounted for. A dress he found in the wagon would have fit none of the victims outside. He had also matched the dead women with every wagon but this one.

Pausing to search a bit longer, he found a family Bible. Inside the cover were listed the names and dates of a man, a deceased woman, and a girl—Deana Shaw, twenty years old. She was the missing victim.

Since animals would soon be investigating the smell of death, Kit felt he had no alternative but to dig a mass grave for all the bodies. Gathering what papers and photographs he could find, he hoped that someone could identify the dead and notify their next of kin.

It was completely dark by the time Kit laid the last body to rest. Leaning on his shovel, he paused to wipe his brow with his bandanna. Then he removed his hat and bowed his head, searching for the right words.

"Lord, I reckon these folks were the usual mixture of good and bad. Anyway, You knew them a whole lot better than me, so I'll entrust their care to You. I pray You'll let me find the missing girl alive and get her safely back to her kin. Amen."

"That's right pretty." Al Squash's harsh voice broke the stillness of the night.

Kit spun around, but there were three guns on him, so he had no chance to draw. Instead he faced Al squarely. The triumphant sneer on the man's face told Kit what was in store for him. "I don't suppose you boys came along to help me bury these people," he said. "As I see it, you're the ones responsible for their deaths."

Al smiled mockingly. "I don't know what you're talking about, Montgomery. The way I hear it, you're the only hope for peace and harmony in the West. You must not be doing a very good job."

Kit knew he had no chance to draw against four men. He'd be dead before his own gun cleared its holster. He held on to the shovel and watched for an opening. "So what's the game, Squash?"

Al sized him up slowly. "You're a fair-sized man, Montgomery—nearly as big as me. That ought to make a fight between us about even."

"Except for the fact that I've been working for two hours solid, digging this grave and burying sixteen people. I'd say that gives you a considerable edge."

Al waved a hand to dismiss the argument. "You walloped me pretty good last night, Montgomery. That ought to make the fight about even."

Kit knew a fight would only lead to his own death. Win or lose, he would get a beating and be staked out for the vultures. Al Squash had not said so, but it was easy to read in his eyes. Kit leaned on the shovel, as if gathering his strength.

Al shrugged out of his short buffalo coat. Even as he was doing so, Kit scooped up a spadeful of dirt. In a single motion, he swung the shovel—tossing dirt into the faces of the three other trappers. At the same time, he hurled the shovel at Al.

Kelly and the other two either ducked or shut their eyes against the flying dirt. His action offered Kit only the slimmest chance of escape, but he took it.

Darting off into the dark, Kit ran a zigzag course, racing between two wagons. He jumped a clump of sage as the men opened fire. Bullets screamed past his head, kicked up dust on either side of him, and ricocheted off the rocks along his path. He purposely ran in the direction opposite his horse, for Al and the others probably hadn't seen where it was picketed. He would circle the area to reach his mount. It was his only chance to escape.

The shouts of his pursuers grew less audible as Kit left the wagons behind. He still had his handgun, a fact that would slow any search, as few men would blindly chase an adversary who might well blow their brains out.

As he rushed past a tall creosote bush, Kit dived for cover. Then he pulled his gun and waited, breathing hard but trying to hide the sound. He strained his ears for sounds of movement in the night. He could see only a few feet in any direction. If the moon didn't rise too quickly, he might work his way around to his horse and escape.

The minutes ticked away. He heard distant voices once, but saw no target. The night was cool and completely black. Kit had no idea where the four men were. Finally he crawled to a lower stand of brush that wouldn't look like a place of concealment.

After a few more minutes, Kit started to circle back around the wagons. Crouched over, he walked several feet and then paused. His gun was in his hand, ready for instant action. His ears searched the darkness, while he himself was careful not to make a sound or stir up any dust. Al might well have spread out his men in a wide perimeter, forcing Kit to slip through their line. Patience was his best weapon as he painstakingly moved a few feet at a time.

Kit reached the rear of the last wagon and waited, stretching out flat on the ground. He noted two shadows moving toward each other, and concluded that he'd been right between them. He didn't move but turned his gun in their direction. Holding his breath, he could pick up their words.

"I'll bet that hombre headed for the tall timber," Curray was saying in a hushed voice.

"Al still thinks his horse is nearby. We'd have heard him ride off, if he'd escaped," Mole replied.

"Al is letting this jasper get the best of him, Mole. I think we're crazy to be out here in Iron Claw's territory."

"No one is holding you here, Curray. If you want out, get your horse and git."

"That would be the smart move, all right,"

Curray replied. "Too bad I ain't all that smart."

"Let's just drift back to the other end and put on a pot of coffee," Mole suggested. "Montgomery ain't going to attack the four of us."

"I'm for that," Curray said, sounding relieved. "We can pick up Montgomery's trail in the morning. He can run only so far. We'll get him."

Kit lifted his head enough to watch the two men wander back past the wagons, where he figured Al and Kelly must be. Crouching, he slowly crossed the open ground toward his horse. He'd been lucky to escape—darn lucky. Al wouldn't give him another such chance. Next time he would either have to kill the four men or be killed himself. That was not a happy thought.

Then Kit remembered the missing woman. Iron Claw might yet be willing to barter his hostage. If he didn't kill Kit on sight, there might still be a way to negotiate her release. And dealing with Iron Claw might also rid him of Al Squash and his band. It was worth a try.

Chapter Five

Deana watched the Indian eat a quick breakfast of roots, berries, and some dried meat. He didn't offer her anything, and she was smart enough not to ask. She was content to drink from the small spring until she couldn't swallow another drop.

Iron Claw didn't put the rope around her neck this time. He tied it around her waist. She soon learned why. The terrain was mountainous, one long hill after another, and soon she was climbing steep escarpments, scrambling over tall ridges, and edging along steep cliffs. It was strenuous, exhausting work, and only the help of the horse pulling her along got her up many of the treacherous grades.

By the time the sun was high in the sky, she was dragging her feet, unable to keep up. Her muscles were stiff and sore, her arms were numb from being bound behind her, her head

41

was pounding from the bruises, and her throat was parched. The heat drained her strength, while the heavy clothes made her feel even hotter. She was gasping for breath, her lungs and chest seared by the constant heat and the physical exertion of climbing the endless maze of hills and ravines.

They crossed a small creek about noon, but Iron Claw paused only long enough for his horse to drink. Deana managed a few precious swallows before she was pulled away. Her gnawing hunger made her look longingly at a patch of wild strawberries underfoot.

The trek seemed never-ending, mile after mile and hill after hill. She fell several times, but Iron Claw refused to let her rest. He cursed her in his native tongue, dragged her a few feet as punishment, and then waited until she managed to get back up. When she lingered, he turned his horse around and prodded her with his lance, jabbing her hard until she regained her feet.

Even walking ten miles or more each day had not prepared Deana for the mountain slopes. The air was thin, the sun beat down unmercifully, and she developed blisters on both feet. Her legs ached as though they'd been injected with liquid fire. Every step hurt more than the previous one, each took more effort than the last. The joints in her knees and ankles were in agony, and ragged gasps escaped her lips with every step. At last, when the sun was high overhead, she collapsed.

Iron Claw pulled her several feet over the rocks and through the brush. She rolled her body enough to keep her face out of the dirt and away from the rough stalks of brush. When he stopped, she could not rise. Even when he prodded her with his sharp lance, Deana didn't have the strength to get up again.

"She-dog is weak. Indian squaw walk for days without food or water."

Deana opened her mouth, but her dry, cracked lips couldn't form any words. She slowly shook her head in silent protest.

The Indian grunted in disgust, dismounted, and took hold of her hair. She gasped as he jerked her up to a sitting position. Grimacing, she opened her eyes and looked into his stern face.

"I . . . I can't," she murmured. "I can't go on."

He pulled his large skinning knife and held it to her throat. "I tell you get up, she-dog!"

But she shook her head again. "Even if you kill me, I can't go any farther."

He put the blade against her neck. She held her breath and closed her eyes tightly. Her heart thundered in her chest, as if trying to escape.

With no warning, Iron Claw cut her hands free. Deana opened her eyes in shock. He hadn't slit her throat. She slowly regained her composure, rubbing her chafed wrists.

Iron Claw took her by the arm and lifted her to her feet. Then he swept her up and tossed her onto his horse before swinging up behind her. Neither spoke as they rode for another mile, until the rolling terrain came to the crest of a hill. Beyond it was a sheltered valley. She could see dozens of tepees, hide racks, and campfires. This was Iron Claw's home.

The horse stopped beyond the clearing in the trees. Deana wasn't prepared for the brutal shove that knocked her out of the saddle. She landed hard on the ground.

"Walk, she-dog," the Indian commanded. "You show me that you are weak. I will not show my people that I am weak."

She got up slowly, rubbing her arm and shoulder, bruised from the fall to the ground. With renewed dread, she began to walk toward the camp.

Children and dogs were scampering about, playing games and running after one another. When the youngsters saw her, they began to shout excitedly. The squaws were gathered around the fires, preparing evening meals. As Iron Claw and Deana approached, a number of warriors took notice of her.

Deana was prodded forward by the sharp end of Iron Claw's lance. She hurried her step. He poked her again. She lifted the hem of her skirt and tried to move faster.

The warriors were all watching now. In fact, she was a spectacle for the entire camp. The children shouted and cheered each time Iron Claw jabbed her in the back.

Deana was running, her chest heaving from the effort. The spear struck her again between the shoulders. She tried to get over a stand of wild rose, but it tangled itself in her long dress and she fell flat, barely catching herself on her hands and elbows.

That brought a round of laughter from the children and warriors alike. Her bonnet was jerked off by one daring youngster, and she found herself surrounded by jeering young Indians. Before she could get up, they were at her like a pack of frisky coyote pups.

They threw rocks, jabbed at her with long sticks, and tried to tear away bits of her clothing. She was pinched, swatted, and hit by flying handfuls of grass and dirt. She couldn't see where she was going, because she was trying to protect her face with her hands.

She yelped as one of the children stuck a twisted stick into her hair and yanked it back. She batted at the long branches with her hands, trying to get away from the brutal teasing. All around her was an ocean of ridicule and hate. Tears filled her eyes, but she kept walking toward the camp.

Quite without warning, the children fell silent and moved aside as a tall Indian came forward to confront her and Iron Claw. He spoke heatedly, shouting in anger while pointing at Deana.

Iron Claw dismounted and boldly stood up to the other man. He replied in even, subdued tones, not offering to lose his own temper. That seemed to infuriate the other man even more.

Awkwardly standing alone, Deana was trembling from the hostile treatment. She quickly took note of the scrape on one arm and the shredded condition of her dress. Her tangled hair hung in her face, and she could feel the wetness of a slight trickle of blood running down her back. Iron Claw's lance was sharp.

The hostile brave took a step toward Deana. He pointed at her again and shouted at Iron Claw. She didn't understand his words, but she didn't like his vicious sneer. When his malevolent eyes rested on her, she cringed inwardly.

"You are mine!" he said in English. "I put claim to you!"

Deana involuntarily stepped back, fearful at once. The man facing her was her worst nightmare come to life. Whatever his race, he would have looked savage. His braided hair was in ornamented locks hanging almost to his waist. He had dark, extremely bushy eyebrows; yellow, jagged teeth; and a large, flat nose. His deep-set eyes, above hard, protruding cheekbones, were overshadowed by a prominent forehead. Below a colorfully decorated breastplate, he wore a large pendant dangling on a leather thong about his neck. His right ear was pierced, decorated with a gold earring.

"I am Puma," he said self-importantly. "I am war chief."

"She is my captive," Iron Claw reminded Puma.

"I am your brother," Puma shouted angrily. "You will give her to me!"

"It is for me to decide."

"Tribal law gives a captive woman to all warriors. I will take her for my own!"

Iron Claw shook his head. "No. Little Deer can do no work. White she-dog will serve me."

The ugly brave glared at his brother, then at Deana. "I have you, you bet. Little Deer is heavy with child. Once baby come . . . then I take you for my bride!"

"It is for me to decide," Iron Claw maintained, meeting his brother's hostile stare.

Deana stood frozen in place, afraid to draw a breath. When Puma looked at her once more, his eyes were ablaze with a hateful fury. She flinched as he reached out quickly and caught a handful of her hair, crushing it within his grasp. He drew her toward him until she was only inches away.

"White woman give me the power," he hissed. "I will beat you and make you good wife, you bet."

Her stomach tied itself into a knot, as icy prickles of fear climbed up her spine. She could see a sadistic brutality in the man's eyes. This was someone who enjoyed hurting others. He tossed the hair into her face and strode across the camp.

Deana's lodging for the night was a pole buried in the ground next to Iron Claw's painted tepee. She was bound to it with a rope so short that she was able to sit down but not stretch out or get comfortable. It was a popular spot for a while, as the children came to torment her. By the time the camp slept, she was covered with scratches and bruises. She was hungry and thirsty, but no one offered her anything. Rather than incur the wrath of Iron Claw, she kept her misery to herself.

Twisting around to face the post that held her, she tried to find a position in which she could at least doze off. It was impossible, for her arms were held up until her wrists were even with her head, and the pole was too small to lean against. She finally gave up, tucking her chin against one shoulder and trying to relax. She was half asleep when she heard footsteps.

Looking up, she saw moccasined feet. Puma was standing over her, his eyes full of malice.

"White squaw must be thirsty," he said with mock concern. When she didn't reply, his eyes narrowed to tiny slits. "I can help you, white woman."

Deana certainly didn't want help from Puma. Any assistance he might offer would surely be more harm than help. Unable to do anything else, she leaned away from him, pulling back as far as she could from his menacing gaze.

He grinned at her, but there was no warmth in his face. She saw that he was holding a flask in one hand and a piece of half-cooked meat in the other.

"Are you thirsty, white woman?"

She didn't know what to do. If she said no, he might take that as an insult. If she said yes, he would see her as weak. He took her hesitation as some kind of answer.

"Here you are," he said with a laugh, tipping the flask up over her. The water poured onto her head, dousing her face and the front of her bodice. His laughter echoed through the night.

Deana blinked at the water in her eyes. She wondered if she dare call out to Iron Claw. He and his pregnant wife were inside the tent. She needed only to shout for him.

"White woman," Puma hissed, putting his face down close to hers, "you will give me the power. I will have you for my wife, you bet."

"Why do you want me?" Having found her voice, she risked speaking to him. "Why do you want a white wife?"

He grinned. "You will give me the power, white woman. Iron Claw is weak. I will lead my people to glory."

"But I've never done anything to the Indian people. Why me?"

He didn't seem to hear her question. Instead, he pulled out a large skinning knife and held it before her eyes. The flask was at her feet, forgotten. He used the knife to slice a piece of meat. Then he teasingly took a bite of it and chewed slowly.

"White woman is hungry. If you tell my brother that you want me, I will let you eat."

Again she was faced with a terrible dilemma. If she refused, it would be an affront. If she accepted, she would be bound by her word. She ducked her head and refused to answer.

The knife appeared before her eyes. She swallowed the scream that jumped into her throat. When she looked up at Puma, she was terrified. His smile was that of a madman.

"If I cut off your nose, no one else will want you—ever. Then you would be glad to call me your husband."

"N-no!" she gasped. "Please, no!"

"Cry out and I will kill you," he warned her.

Deana was too frightened even to breathe. The knife glistened in the firelight. She closed her eyes and awaited the horrible fate that Puma had planned for her.

Chapter Six

"**I**ron Claw won't like what you're doing, Puma," a man's voice declared. "Torturing a prisoner is the right of the chief, not a second-rate warrior like you."

Kit saw the girl open her eyes and immediate relief flood her features, but he couldn't watch her long. The Indian had turned to face him, knife still in hand, poised to strike.

"Soldier Kit is a fool!" he growled. "I will kill you for entering our camp!"

"Iron Claw wouldn't like that either, Puma. I've come to speak to him."

"My brother is weak. He does not know an enemy from a friend!"

"Are you willing to challenge him over my visit?" Kit asked.

Puma considered the idea. He glared hard at Kit, the desire to attack and kill him shining in his eyes. But he was not foolish enough to defy Iron Claw openly. Restraining himself, he backed down. "He is chief—for now. I will see what my brother say."

"Good. You're smarter than I gave you credit for."

The Indian glowered at the girl. She recoiled from him, pulling back against the cords that bound her to the pole. Naked fear shone on her face as Puma pointed a warning finger at her.

"Remember, white woman, you will be mine. If Soldier Kit take you away, you will both die."

"You've got her scared, Puma. Why don't you go kick a dog? That ought to make you feel important."

Though not as big as Kit, Puma was stoutly built, and obviously he wasn't afraid of any white man. "One day I will kill you, Soldier Kit."

"You may try, Puma, but I won't be as easy to kill as the women and children you've slaughtered."

Puma clenched his fists, longing to attack with his knife. But he held his temper in check. With an angry glance back at the girl, he stormed across the camp.

Kit watched him stride away. He knew that Puma hated all whites and that if not for Iron Claw, there would have been endless bloodshed between the Owatawna and the settlers. But although Puma might well try to kill Kit, it wouldn't be until the white man left camp. Iron Claw was chief, and Puma had to show respect for the leader of their tribe. It was the Indian way.

"M-mister?" the girl whispered.

Still watching Puma, Kit held up a hand to silence the girl momentarily. Once he was convinced that the Indian would offer them no trouble, he turned to her.

"Better not speak except to answer my questions," he told her quietly. "I'm here to help if I can."

She sagged against the rope, hardly able to hold up her head. Kit could see that she'd taken a lot of punishment.

"Can you walk?" he asked.

Her eyes lit up. "You give me a chance to escape, and I'll run like a deer."

In spite of their desperate situation, Kit smiled. The girl had spirit. "Have you eaten today?" he asked.

She shook her head. "Not since I was captured yesterday."

Kit didn't like her answer. In the event of a running battle, she would be too weak to keep up. He wished that he had thought to bring food. Feeling his shirt pocket, he found that he still had two strips of jerky left. He fed them to the girl and gave her several swallows of water from his flask.

"I'm sorry it's so little, but if Puma saw me give you food and water, he'd have reason enough to attack me. A prisoner belongs to the tribe. It is forbidden for me to interfere."

"I understand," she said softly.

"I can't do anything more for you tonight."

She swallowed hard. "If . . . if you can't help me get away," she said softly, "don't leave me to become Puma's woman. I'd prefer death."

He didn't reply to that. What could he have said? He took another look around. No one appeared to be watching, but this didn't give him any false feelings of security. A wrong move could jeopardize his chances of getting her out of camp or even surviving. He had to be content that he'd driven off Puma and slipped her something to eat and drink.

"Keep your hopes up, little lady. I'll try to get you out of this mess tomorrow. Iron Claw won't want to deal, but I've got something he wants. If he doesn't kill me on sight, we might both get out of this place alive."

The girl didn't reply, but she looked at him imploringly. She had plenty of grit, he thought. She hadn't quit yet, and she'd taken some rough treatment. Kit didn't know why Puma had claimed her. That complication was going to make a difficult job even harder, but he would do what he could.

He left the girl alone, taking the flask with him. The Owatawna camp was not totally alien to him. He knew he could sleep in a hut used for guests. Most of the warriors had seen him around the fires, and he had dealt with Iron Claw a number of times. They weren't friends, but they'd come to respect each other. It was to his advantage that they had both profited from their relationship. That might tip the scales in his favor.

Kit found the hut occupied by an old Indian sleeping on one side of the dead fire pit. In spite of the danger, Kit felt safer in the Indian camp than out where he could be tracked down by Al Squash and his friends. They weren't going to come into Iron Claw's camp looking for him. If Puma didn't decide to kill him during the night, he might get a few hours of sleep.

Kit was up before daylight, but he remained quiet, aloof, and patient. Iron Claw would know that he was in camp, so he left the next move up to the chief. Taking up a place near his horse, Kit took out his skinning knife and began to whittle on a thick tree branch. The girl was awake, but she had the good sense not to pay much attention to him.

Iron Claw stepped out of his tepee and surveyed the girl and the camp. Finally he looked at Kit, giving him no greeting or friendly gesture, only a long, hard gaze. Kit looked up impassively from his whittling, meeting the chief on his own terms.

Puma was not so discreet, striding boldly across the camp to meet the chief face to face. They exchanged some heated words in their native tongue, but Kit couldn't understand what was being said. From the girl's expression, neither could she. But it was obvious to Kit that he and she were the subject of the conversation. It was fortunate for them that it was Iron Claw, and not his hateful brother, who ruled the Owatawna.

After a time, Puma left, and Iron Claw approached Kit. He offered no form of greeting.

"Soldier Kit is not a wise man. My brother wants to kill you."

"Puma may have learned the white man's tongue as well as you, Iron Claw. But he does not know us like the great chief of the Owatawna."

"Why do you come, Soldier Kit?"

"I'm no longer a soldier, Iron Claw. I left

the fort and the Army. I don't work for anyone now."

The chief narrowed his gaze. "Why do you come to my camp? White men kill my sister and five others. I will make whites pay."

"You've done that already," Kit pointed out. "I buried the sixteen people you killed at the edge of the plains. Those were innocent travelers."

Iron Claw didn't deny it. "Maybe Soldier Kit die too."

"Maybe," Kit said carefully. "And maybe I can deal with a man who knows that killing innocent people is not true revenge. For that you must destroy the men who killed your sister and the other members of your tribe."

Iron Claw frowned. "You know these men?"

"I know where they are now," Kit replied.

The chief straightened at once. "You will tell me, Soldier Kit."

Kit put away his skinning knife and tossed away the trimmed branch. "I will tell you . . . for a price."

The light of understanding entered the chief's eyes. "You want the white she-dog."

"I do. While you have her, the Army will hunt and kill your people. I can stop that from happening. You don't want a war you cannot win against the white people."

Iron Claw shook his head. "Little Deer too big with child to do chores. I would have the white woman work for her."

"And then you will give her to Puma," Kit added. "He will treat her very badly."

"Puma want the power that comes with having white woman. I cannot stop him."

Kit shrugged. "I thought that you were chief, Iron Claw. Now you tell me that Puma runs your camp. I should have spoken to him."

Iron Claw's eyes grew hard with anger. "You tell me white men who kill my sister!"

But Kit crossed his arms stubbornly. "I'm talking a trade, Chief. I can tell you where those men are, but you must pay the price. They are only a few miles away."

The chief frowned. "I torture you, Soldier Kit. You would tell."

"I might," Kit agreed. "And I might lie with my dying breath."

The chief looked thoughtful, staring off into space. When he spoke, his words were full of longing and melancholy.

"Many winters past, we fight only other tribes for the buffalo. We ride free like wind. We take from land what we need, then move our camp. Now we run from the soldiers, hide like the hunted animal. You have taken our lives and made us feel hate and shame."

"Killing innocent people isn't the answer, Iron Claw. The white man's army is mighty, with as many men as the grains of sand in the desert. You must learn to share the land and live with them in peace. Otherwise, you and your people will all perish."

"I am chief . . . for now," the Indian said softly. "Puma would take warriors and attack all whites. I kill only to repay the deaths of my people."

"But those were the wrong people, Chief. Give me the girl, and I'll set you after the men who deserve the punishment. They are my enemies too. They would start a war that would kill many people on both sides. If our law was just, we would hang them for their crime."

"Is no crime for white man to kill Indian."

"It will be one day soon. Both sides must learn to live by rules, Iron Claw, and neither should kill the other for sport or revenge."

Iron Claw seemed to consider the logic of Kit's words. After a few moments, he looked over at the girl. His jaw was grimly set when he again met Kit's eyes.

"Puma will not let you have the white woman. If you take her, he will follow. He will kill."

"I'll take my chances against your brother, Chief. Send him after the men who killed your sister and the others. Then I'll take the girl and leave. You can tell him I stole her."

Iron Claw shook his head. "I not lie to him. He will follow you like shadow. He will find you."

"Then it will be between Puma and me," Kit told the chief. "Let me take the girl, and I'll tell you what you want to know."

Iron Claw hesitated briefly, then nodded. "You take white she-dog. Wait for Puma to leave camp. You run fast, Soldier Kit. Never come back."

"I'll do that."

"You come as friend, you leave as friend." The chief's expression grew dark and stern. "You will be friend no longer. If again I see you, Soldier Kit, I will kill."

"I understand, Iron Claw."

The chief stared hard at him for a long moment. Then he called out to Puma and some of the other braves, who gathered around him and Kit. "Soldier Kit know who kill our people," the chief told Puma. "You will take warriors and find them."

"I don't believe white man!" Puma hissed, glaring suspiciously at Kit.

Iron Claw raised a hand to silence him. "We will see if he tell truth. If he lie, we will kill him."

Puma's face lit up. Obviously he'd rather cut Kit's throat than find the four trappers who'd murdered his sister.

"Where are these men?" Iron Claw asked Kit.

"There are four of them—trappers. They are the ones who hunt and kill your animals up in the Little Bear country. Their names are Al Squash, Curray Walters, Kelly Holden, and Mole Kinnes. They carry traps and furs."

"I have seen these men before," Puma said. "How do you know that they killed our sister and the others?"

"Al Squash showed your people's scalps at the fort. I fought with him, and now they are after me. They are on the trail back in the hills."

Puma stared at Kit suspiciously. "These men hunt for you. How do we know that they killed our sister? Maybe you wish only to be rid of them."

"They have the scalps among their furs. You will find the hair of your sister. Do you want the guilty men or not?"

"Take braves and find them," Iron Claw ordered. "I will watch for signal. We will trap them."

Puma turned, but stopped at once, nodding toward Kit. "What about Soldier Kit?"

"He will wait. If he lie, we kill."

That satisfied Puma. He beckoned to some of the warriors and hurried off. As soon as he was out of hearing range, Iron Claw turned to Kit.

"Be swift like running deer, Soldier Kit. Puma will hunt you."

Kit nodded. "I will remember you as an honorable man, Chief Iron Claw. I hope one day there will be peace."

"Better that we never meet," he answered. "When next I see you, you die."

Kit didn't reply. As soon as Puma had ridden away from camp, Kit headed for his own horse. He would have a few hours of head start, but it wouldn't be much against a man like Puma, who would pursue Kit to the ends of the earth.

Chapter Seven

The girl regarded him anxiously, but Kit had no time to reassure her as he calmly led Dusky across the camp and stopped beside Iron Claw's tepee.

"A-are you . . . are you leaving me?" she asked him hesitantly.

Kit surveyed the camp once more. Puma was gone, but he might have instructed one of his trusted warriors to keep an eye on both Kit and the girl. If he got word that he'd been tricked, he would be back in moments—not a very pleasant prospect.

Looking down at the girl, Kit was struck by how frail and weak she appeared. But there was an alertness to her, an underlying courage. She was beaten, but not defeated.

After a final glance around, Kit dropped quickly to her side. He took out his skinning knife to cut her bonds. Instantly alarm sprang into the young woman's eyes, and she turned her head away fearfully. It occurred to him that she expected him to end her suffering. He pretended not to notice, cutting her free. As she sighed with relief, he looked her over.

"Can you stand up?"

She grimaced as she tried to get up. "I . . . I'm rather stiff, but. . . ."

He didn't dare waste any time. He put one arm under her and lifted her up, swinging her into the saddle on Dusky's back. He was quickly up behind her and turned the horse toward the trees beyond the camp.

Once out of sight of the tepees, he pushed the game little horse hard, heading toward the next range of mountains, the Little Bear country. If he could convince Puma that he'd headed in that direction, the man might commit himself to trying to cut them off. That would allow Kit time to reverse his direction and head for the open plains. A way station and a few ranches were not more than fifty miles away. All Kit needed was a full day's head start, and Puma would never set eyes on the girl again.

Kit dismounted frequently and walked with the horse, managing a fair pace for an hour before riding for a short spell. He repeated this process all day.

"It isn't fair," the girl argued during a short rest stop. "I can walk. I'm the one trying to escape. I should be helping you."

But he had examined her blistered feet. It was a wonder she could even stand. "Puma doesn't care who's helping whom. Once he finds out that I've taken you, he'll be hot on our trail."

She didn't argue his point. He gave her a couple of hard rolls and some beef jerky to eat, and she sipped frequently from the canteen. She'd have to wait for a decent meal until they stopped for the night. He had to admire her, as she didn't complain one bit.

Kit pushed the horse and himself, resting only for the sake of the animal. They continued until well after dark, going as long as Kit could make out landmarks. When they reached a small stream, he followed it. A mile or so later, he decided the horse would have to rest.

He fixed cold beans and opened a tin of pears. It was not a feast, but the girl ate what he gave her and did whatever he instructed her to do. He put the ground blanket down for her, but she sat on the edge of the bank and soaked her feet in the stream, using a wet handkerchief to wash her face and arms.

Kit held his rifle on his lap as he sat on a fallen log. He listened to the sounds of the night and watched the young woman. It had been so long since he'd been alone with a member of the opposite sex, he couldn't remember how to talk to one of them. He and this girl had nothing in common but a ruthless enemy.

"You'd better get some sleep," he told her quietly. "We'll have to cover fifty miles tomorrow. There won't be any time for resting along the way."

She looked over her shoulder at him and dried her feet. Then she sat down on the ground blanket. He stared off into the night and tried not to pay any attention to her.

"Who are you?" she asked. "How did you get Iron Claw to let me go?"

"My name's Kit Montgomery. I bartered some information for your release."

"What kind of information?"

"The attack against you folks was in retaliation for the killing of some Owatawna. I told Iron Claw the names of the men who killed his people."

"My name is Deana Shaw," she said. "I forgot to introduce myself at our first meeting."

He grinned at that. "It was more important to escape with our hair intact."

"Speaking of hair. . . ." She unhappily ran her fingers through hers. "Mine could use about a week of washing and brushing."

"I've got a comb in my saddlebags, but the only brush I have is for my horse."

"A curry brush would probably suit me, but I'd prefer the loan of your comb."

Kit retrieved his comb and handed it to Deana. She began to work it through the tangles, pulling and tugging at the knotted strands.

"You've had a rough time of it," Kit said. "You were lucky that Iron Claw wanted you to help his pregnant wife with her work. Most of the Owatawna prisoners aren't so fortunate."

She paused to look over her ragged attire. She was covered with scratches and bruises, her dress was shredded in places, and she was stiff and sore in every muscle in her body.

"I'm fortunate that you came," she said shortly. "I don't know how much more I could have taken. I've never seen such—such hatred from even the children. They took delight in making me cry out."

"They were taking out on you their anger against the white men who killed their people. It isn't right, but it's understandable."

"You seem to defend the Indians." There was a hint of challenge in her voice.

"No, ma'am. I don't condone killing anyone because of his race—white or Indian."

"I didn't mean. . . ."

"I know. I wouldn't fault you for hating the Indians, considering what they've done to you."

She continued to work on her tangles in silence. He had the feeling that she was embarrassed at having him watch, but it was hard to take his eyes off her. She was a modest, decent sort of girl, who'd suffered the discomforts of the day without a single complaint, not once asking anything of him.

Kit went over to his saddlebags and dug out his spare shirt and pants. She looked up as he dropped them next to her on the blanket.

"These might be a little big for you, but wearing them will be better than having your bare skin rubbing against the inside of the stirrups. I imagine your, uh, legs are raw."

She smiled at his quick flush of embarrassment. "Thank you, Mr. Montgomery. I'll put them on in the morning."

He turned his back on her, looking out into the dark. The only sounds he could hear belonged to the night.

"Aren't you going to sleep?" she asked.

"I'll doze off from time to time. I imagine we're safe enough for the time being."

"I haven't gotten around to telling you how grateful I am, Mr. Montgomery." Deana's voice was soft and warmly sincere. "To be truthful, I don't know how to thank someone who risks his own life to save mine. I wish that I. . . ."

"Don't fret about it, Miss Shaw," he said, cutting her gratitude short. "I haven't saved you yet."

"All the same, I think you are a very brave man, Kit Montgomery. And—no matter what happens—I still thank you from the bottom of my heart."

"Go to sleep," he growled, embarrassed.

Deana relaxed on the ground blanket and covered herself with the single cover. He glanced in her direction as she closed her eyes and pulled the blanket up around her shoulders.

"I won't think it improper of you if you sleep next to me, Mr. Montgomery. It'll be cold before morning."

"I'll remember that," he told her dryly, knowing full well that he would face the chill of night alone.

Deana forced her eyes open. After going so long without sleep or proper rest, doing so was a real chore. The sky was growing light, but it was the crackling of a fire and the smell of frying salt pork that had aroused her. She saw

Kit Montgomery a few feet away. His back was to her as he watched over the meal, so she was able to appraise him without his knowing it.

He was a bit taller than average, with strong shoulders and muscular arms, and he moved with a natural grace. His hair was dark brown, as were his eyes. A square jaw and slender nose offset his rather narrow lips. The confidence in his manner implied that he was a man who wouldn't back down easily.

Her thoughts shifted to their uncertain future. Even if they managed to get away, what would she do? She had no family or relations to turn to. Even her friends were hundreds of miles away. She supposed she could get a job to earn her keep, but she knew very little about the West.

And what would Kit Montgomery expect from her? He had risked his life to save hers and had even made a deadly enemy of Puma— not a matter to be taken lightly—all for her sake. What if he expected or wanted more of her than she was willing to give?

Shrugging away such thoughts, she pulled the pair of pants under the blanket and put them on, tucking the remnants of her under-skirt inside the waistband. When she put the shirt over her bodice, it was so baggy that she could have fit a second person inside. She decided that Kit was bigger than she had first thought.

She wondered if he'd managed to get any sleep. She knew he hadn't gotten under the blanket with her. Now that she had gotten a good night's sleep, she would be able to keep a vigil while he slept.

"Should we be risking a fire?" she asked, folding the blanket.

Kit had been considering the different routes they might take. The girl's voice gave him a start.

"Anyone close enough to smell our fire would already know we were here. This shaved bark doesn't give off any smoke, so it won't be seen."

"I didn't know that," Deana admitted. "I guess you must be very smart about surviving out here in the wilderness."

Kit shrugged. "Some things are common sense. A person is only as smart as he is knowledgeable about his surroundings."

"You talk like a philosopher, Mr. Montgomery."

"Only stating a fact. A college professor would probably be a dummy out here—just as I'd be a dummy sitting in his classroom. You can't measure a person's intelligence outside his natural surroundings."

Deana moved over next to the fire and held her hands out to warm them.

"My father was a smart man back home, but I don't think he was fully aware of what would face him out here."

"He knew to keep the Indians from taking you. That shows that he had some savvy."

"What about you, Mr. Montgomery?" she asked, to change the painful subject. "Where do you come from?"

"I was born on a wagon train somewhere on the Iowa plains. My folks settled in Kansas until the war. We lost our farm to rebel neighbors, and I ended up with a bunch of Yankee volunteers. After that I stayed in the Army for a spell. I've been a go-between for the fort the last three years. I often negotiated for hostages and arranged for the release of some Indians as well."

"And have you quit that job?"

"The Department of War decided that too many Indians were making their living by stealing women and children and then selling them back to the Army. A new directive prohibits payment for hostages. That puts me out of a job."

"But you came after me," she said quietly.

"I happened to be the first one at your wagon train, and I figured out that you were not among the dead. Knowing who killed Iron Claw's sister gave me something to bargain with."

"You took a big chance."

He dished up the salt pork and handed a plate to the girl. "I felt that Iron Claw would listen to me."

"And Puma?"

Kit glanced at her. In the light, he could see the misty blue of her eyes. Aside from a mark or two on her face from the punishment she'd received at the hands of the Indians, she was not all that hard to look at. His scrutiny brought a hint of blush to the girl's cheeks, but she didn't look away.

"Puma will come after us," he said flatly. "He will want to kill me, and his plans for you are far worse."

Deana bit her lower lip. "You won't let him take me . . . alive, I mean?"

Kit shook his head. "Puma will never lay a hand on you, Miss Shaw. I'm going to get you to safety before he even knows you're gone."

She gave him a timorous smile, the first he'd seen on her face. He knew his boast might be idle, but the reward of the smile was a new incentive to see that Puma didn't get Deana—not alive, at any rate.

Chapter Eight

Kelly laid Mole against the rocks, but he knew the man was dying. An arrow was deep in Mole's chest, and he'd been shot through the ribs as well. He didn't have long.

"Where the blazes did that bunch come from?" Al cried. "I thought we got away from those buzzards!"

"Must be two parties of them red devils," Kelly said, holding his rifle at the ready position. "I bet Kit Montgomery was in on this."

Al slammed the butt of his rifle against the ground. "That slimy snake sure enough put them dogs on our trail. Blast his miserable hide! We should have killed him that first night!"

"We tried," Kelly reminded him. "We should have shot him the moment we first set eyes on him. Now he's turned the tables on us."

A cry of terror and pain cut the mountain

air, echoing off the hills and vibrating through the trees. It was the death wail of a dying animal—a white man.

"No need to wonder about Curray no more," Al observed. "He should have stuck with us. Three guns had a better chance than one."

"Being last on the trail, he got scared and tried to run," Kelly said. "Now we've got them above and below us. What are we going to do?"

"There's a way out. We'll find it too."

Kelly turned Mole over to check his wounds. He was dead.

"They won't be torturing Mole," Kelly told Al. "Maybe he's the only lucky one among us."

Al barely glanced over at the body. He wet a finger and lifted it to test the direction of the wind. After a moment, he surveyed the terrain. "We've got a chance, Kelly. The wind is with us. Start rounding up some brush. There's a lot of scrub oak and buck brush between us and them Indians. If we can start a fire. . . ."

A few hours later, Iron Claw looked down at the body of the man spread-eagled on the ground. Curray had died an agonizing death.

"What of the others?" he asked Puma.

His brother straightened, nodding toward an area of charred brush and blackened earth.

"There is another in the rocks. He was called Mole."

"I want the one called Squash. He is the leader."

Puma stared out over the burnt-off hillside. "He and another used the fire to escape. We were blocked by the burning brush."

Iron Claw grunted in disgust. "We will follow them. There will be no rest until they are dead."

Puma put a hand on his brother's arm. "What about Soldier Kit and the white squaw? Who is watching them?"

"They are no longer in camp," Iron Claw admitted. "The information about these men was given in exchange for the white she-dog."

Puma's face grew black with fury. "You lied to me! You gave away the white squaw, and she was promised to me!"

Iron Claw shook his head. "The captive was mine, Puma. You asked for her, but I did not agree to give her to you. Soldier Kit gave us the names of the men who killed our sister. Is that not more important than having a white woman be your wife?"

But Puma would not listen to reason. He shoved Iron Claw and reached for his knife. For a moment it appeared he would draw the weapon and attempt to kill his own brother. Then he managed to get control of himself.

"I will find Soldier Kit and kill him. I will have the white squaw."

"We must find the trappers first. They killed our sister and the others. They must die for their crime."

Puma grunted in disgust. "That is job for you. You are chief of tribe. You must find them and kill them. I will take my braves and find Soldier Kit."

"And if I say no?" Iron Claw threw out the challenge.

"Then we will see who commands the warriors," Puma replied evenly. "I have my followers. They will ride with me. If you try to stop me, the tribe will be divided. I do not think you want that to happen."

Iron Claw let him walk away. To challenge him openly would split the loyalty of the warriors. He would let Puma take his followers and go after Soldier Kit and the white woman. Iron Claw would still have enough men to find Squash and avenge the deaths of his sister and the other innocent Owatawna.

He watched with no visible emotion as Puma gathered his group and left. Only eleven rode with his brother, Iron Claw noted with satisfaction. He still had thirty braves at his command. Puma was not so strong as he had feared.

As Puma and his warriors left to find the trail of Soldier Kit and the white woman, Iron Claw felt a deep sadness. So long as he had dealt with the white man from the fort, he'd felt there was hope for peace between Indians and whites. Now there could be no peace.

He thought of the courage of Soldier Kit and the white woman, who had suffered his mistreatment without complaint. She would have been a good Indian squaw, for she had inner strength. As for Soldier Kit, he had risked death to rescue a woman he didn't even know. His death would be a loss to both Indians and whites.

Turning back to the matter at hand, Iron Claw prepared to track down Al Squash, the one responsible for the killings. For that crime he must pay the ultimate price—his life.

Kit paused at the crest of the ridge to look back at the cloud of smoke far across the mountains. He could only speculate about what it meant.

"What's that?" Deana asked, pointing down toward the valley below them.

Shading his eyes, Kit saw several buildings

and corrals. He had guessed their location better than he'd hoped.

"It's the Farleys' ranch. We can get another horse from them."

"You mean they'll help us?"

Kit didn't know the answer to that. "They've been friendly with the Indians since settling in the valley a dozen years back. I don't know if they will welcome us or not. They don't want to hurt their friendship with the Owatawna."

He directed the horse down the slope at an easy pace, conserving Dusky's strength. The animal had carried a double load for many miles without much food or rest, and it was still twenty miles to the way station.

Deana sagged slightly in the saddle, leaning back against Kit's chest. Kit had not had a woman in his arms in a long time. He found he enjoyed being close to her and listening to her soft voice.

Their escape had left little time for small talk, and he realized that he didn't know much about her. She had told him of her father's hopes for a new life and that she had no relatives in the West. He knew that she was in her early twenties and that she was a lady of considerable mettle.

"I haven't asked before," she said after a prolonged silence, "but are you a family man?"

"Like you, I'm alone in the world. There aren't many women at the fort. Single ladies out here have about fifty suitors each, so I haven't met many."

"You said that you were leaving the Army. What are your plans—once we get away from Puma?"

"I haven't given it much thought. I've saved some money over the years, so I could go into dairy farming. There might be a future in it."

"That sounds like a good idea to me, but I've never had to think about working for a living—not until now. I naturally assumed that I would work on Father's farm."

"Any new ideas about your future?" Kit asked.

She looked back at him, but he didn't know what to make of her expression.

"I'd be happy to hear suggestions," she replied hesitantly.

"First things first," Kit said. "You'll have plenty of time to figure things out—after we've escaped from Puma."

Leaving the timberline, they rode into the valley. Before they reached the ranch house, there were three men with rifles on the porch. Kit had met Ira Farley only once, and he didn't really know him. Farley was a heavyset man with thin, white hair and a constant squint. His rifle was pointed in their direction.

"That's close enough," Ira said. He jerked the end of his gun toward the open country. "Just keep moving, Montgomery. We don't need any trouble here."

Kit stopped Dusky and looked past Deana to the three on the porch. A quick glance told him there was to be no welcome from anyone at the Farley ranch.

"All I'm looking for is a second horse, Farley. I can pay you, if you're of a mind to sell."

Ira only tightened his grip on his rifle. "You ain't going to drag me into this private war of yours. Puma sent word that white men had killed several members of their tribe—and he's looking for you. If we were to aid you in any way, it'd be like putting a gun to our own heads."

As he spoke, the door opened behind him, and a woman appeared in the entrance. She peered out at Kit and Deana, then looked at Ira.

"Couldn't we at least give them a meal and another horse, Father?"

Ira shook his head stubbornly. "You're due to give me a grandchild in a few weeks, daughter. Do you want to risk the lives of your husband and your child just to be neighborly?"

Kit could see that the woman was heavy with child. He turned Dusky with the reins.

"I can see the way it is, Farley. We'll ride on."

The old man didn't look very happy. "I'd really like to help you, Montgomery, but I don't dare. Iron Claw has let us alone for three years. We let them have beef and we trade horses from time to time. I can't risk a war with the Owatawna. Puma is only looking for an excuse to kill every white man in the territory."

"I told you I understand," Kit replied. "I'm not blaming you."

"Look at their horse, Father," the young woman said. "That animal is about dead on his feet. Mr. Montgomery and the lady won't make the way station without some kind of help."

One of the men on the porch looked over at Deana and then back at Ira. "I've got two horses, Pa," he said. "Why don't I ride over to the way station and see if we've got any mail?"

Ira frowned. "If Puma catches you, he'll think we're riding with Montgomery."

"The lady needs a horse, Pa. If trouble comes, I'll head for home."

"Jeff is right, Father," the woman said. "It's the only decent thing to do."

The old man looked at his son. The third man—the woman's husband, Kit assumed—didn't offer an opinion, waiting for Ira to make the decision.

"All right. You can take some grub and your own mounts. See that you don't get yourself killed."

Jeff went into the house to gather what he needed.

"Puma is on our trail, so he might soon be along," Kit told them. "Iron Claw shouldn't be following us. He's searching for the men that he knows killed his people."

"If Puma rides in, I'll point him after you. I ain't sticking my neck out for you, Montgomery."

"That's the way I want it. There's no need for anyone else to get hurt."

The woman went into the house and returned a minute later. She handed her husband a bundle and nodded at Kit and Deana.

"Here's an old dress of mine. It isn't much, dear, but it's better than what you're wearing."

"You're very gracious," Deana told her, accepting the clothes.

Jeff appeared with two horses. Deana

mounted one of them, and then they were ready to leave.

"Remember, son," Ira said, "if there's trouble, get back here quick."

"I'll remember, Pa."

Then they rode out of the yard. Though it was still twenty miles to the way station, at least they had a chance to get there before dark. Kit would worry then about what to do with Deana. The way Jeff was looking at her, he wondered if the rancher's son had some ideas of his own.

Oddly enough he felt a pang of jealousy, though he could see no reason for it. He hadn't said a single thing to Deana that could be considered amorous, and she hadn't shown him anything but courtesy and a natural gratitude for saving her life. There was no reason to get jealous over another man's interest in her—but he couldn't deny the feeling. Perhaps it came only from his protective nature, but there was no doubt that he didn't like sharing her.

Chapter Nine

Kelly slid down the rocky shale bank, grunting as he hit the bottom of the hill. Al came lumbering and sliding down next to him, winded and sweating profusely from the effort. He sat down and fanned his face with his hat.

"We can rest a couple of minutes, Kelly. Them red devils must be a few miles behind us."

Kelly took a long look around. "The road for the stagecoach is only half a mile away. We've got to catch that coach, or we'll be dead by morning."

Al's face was flushed from the exercise. He flexed his shoulders to ease his tired muscles. Then he stared in the direction of the main road. "What makes you so sure the stage is still running? Them Indians might have scared them off by now."

"Killing those Owatawna is what stirred up

this trouble. The news hasn't had time to spread yet, so my guess is that the stage will be running as usual."

"Stinking savages," Al said heatedly. "I wish I'd never set eyes on them Owatawna."

"Curray and Mole would sure agree with you."

"It's all that Montgomery's fault. I'll bet you next winter's pelts that he put those Indians on our trail."

"That man has been nothing but trouble," Kelly agreed.

"I'll get even with that dirty dog someday. He can't run forever. When our paths cross again, I'm going to kill him—slow and brutal, the way those savages killed Curray."

Kelly jerked his head around and listened. "The coach is coming! I can hear it!"

Al jumped to his feet and gazed up the valley. "There's an escort of troopers with it." He laughed. "First time in my life I was ever glad to see them blue-bellies!"

Al and Kelly began running for their lives— incentive enough to keep them going.

Iron Claw could also see the approaching stage and the outriders. He was still two miles away, with several steep hills between him and the open valley floor. He saw that there was no way to intercept the two men before they reached the stage.

Two Hands, Iron Claw's best warrior, rode up beside his chief and looked down over the valley. "We've lost them," he said in their native tongue.

"There are only a few soldiers. We can stop their escape," Iron Claw said firmly.

Two Hands let out a long breath. "The horses are tired. We have had no rest during the night. It may be too much for the braves."

"If we do not catch them, there will be war. We attack."

Once he knew Iron Claw had made up his mind, Two Hands didn't argue. He considered their situation.

"We can catch them at the end of the valley, where the stage crosses the stream," Two Hands suggested. "There is a trail through the hills. It will mean a running fight, but we might stop them."

Iron Claw stared out at the stage and riders. There were eight soldiers, plus the guard and any others inside. A major battle would be necessary to take trappers Al Squash and Kelly, since the soldiers would protect them.

"Get started, Two Hands. It will take all our speed to get to the crossing ahead of them."

Two Hands turned his horse and gave the

orders. Though tired, the warriors moved out together. Iron Claw had good men, brave warriors all. He regretted the decision to attack, for after the battle there would be orphans and widows in the camp.

For a long moment, he thought of the man Soldier Kit. He was a man to be trusted. There were many such white men; only those like Al Squash started wars.

He wondered if Puma had caught up with the white woman and Soldier Kit. There would be no rest for any of them until her fate was settled. If Soldier Kit had no woman, she would make him a fine squaw. If Puma took her, she would kill either him or herself. She was not the kind to submit to a man like Puma.

Led by Two Hands, the braves rode in single file along the narrow trail. They hoped to get to Squash before the stage reached the safety of the way station, where there would be more men and a harder fight.

Jeff rode alongside Deana, talking with her as if they were long-lost friends. He was a cheerful sort who had a way with words. By the time they had gone five miles, he'd had her laughing more than once.

Kit, on the other hand, was watching out for Puma. He kept the pace as fast as his game horse could manage. He didn't have time for conversation, but he listened.

"It's a nice place to live," Jeff was telling Deana. "We've a herd of cattle, fifty head of horses, and streams and ponds that are full of trout."

"It must be beautiful." Deana sounded impressed.

"There's a quiet little spot I'm fond of," Jeff went on. "I'll build my home there one of these days. It's down near the freshwater stream and sits back in the trees, sheltered on three sides by the mountains. I'll be able to pipe water into the house, and I intend to buy a stove with a heater for the water. My wife will have hot water available right in the kitchen."

"How wonderful!" Deana exclaimed. "I saw one of those stoves back home in the most luxurious house in town. They had a pump right in the kitchen and used a reservoir tank for hot water. It must be wonderful to be able to run water for a hot bath without heating it by the bucket."

"Pa and Howie—that's my brother-in-law—will help me build the house. We've got several hired hands who will pitch in too. I could have the place set up by winter."

"Doesn't that sound like a beautiful place, Kit?"

Kit was so busy scanning the horizon, he was hardly aware that she was speaking to him. He was surprised that she used his first name, and didn't answer immediately.

"I bet Kit wouldn't know how to live with a roof over his head," Jeff said good-naturedly. "He's been roughing it so long that four walls might give him bad dreams."

"Is that right, Kit?" Deana once more tried to bring him into the conversation.

"Probably," he said dryly.

"What are your plans, Deana?" Jeff was already using the lady's first name. That grated on Kit's nerves. He'd saved her from Puma and the Owatawna, and yet he didn't take such liberties.

"I don't really know. Everything has been uncertain since the Indian attack on our wagons. I haven't had time to do any planning for the future. Getting away from the Owatawna is all I've been thinking about. If not for Kit—"

"You're quite a remarkable woman," Jeff said, cutting her short. "Not many people could have withstood the treatment of those Indians and still be able to smile. I think you're the kind of woman the West needs."

What a line of hogwash, Kit thought. He knew the words were true, but it was patronizing to say things like that. Surely Deana must see through Jeff's feeble efforts to impress her. She couldn't be gullible enough to be taken in by a few well-chosen words.

Kit rode stiffly erect, his lips drawn in a thin line. He should have ridden around Ira's place. Who needed Jeff Farley along, anyway? They'd been doing just fine without him.

He nudged Dusky with his heels. The horse was laboring, but he found some second wind and picked up the pace. The increased speed made it more difficult to talk back and forth, for they were dodging brush and sage along the valley floor.

Jeff kept up, however, somehow managing to stick right with Deana. They continued to talk as if they were the best of friends. It was enough to make a full-grown man sick to his stomach, Kit thought. How did Jeff know what to say to a woman he'd just met? How could he be so at ease with her? How could Kit ever compete with a guy like him?

Chapter Ten

The people at the stage way station were hospitable and greeted them all with open arms. Deana was given a chance to take a bath and change into the clothes Ira's daughter had given her. Jeff made himself right at home, while Kit saw to the needs of Dusky and the other two horses.

"Been on the move, son?" The old hostler was near the barn, working on a broken harness.

"You might say that," Kit answered wryly.

"We got word that there might be Injun trouble. Soldiers are escorting the stage and any freight wagons going through. Haven't had to do that for a spell."

"Puma and Iron Claw are looking for the men who killed their sister and a few other Owatawna. They know the ones they're after."

"Never had no trouble with Iron Claw," the

97

old man said thoughtfully. "But that Puma is a crazy one. No telling about him."

"I agree."

"My name's Joe Clue. I already know you by reputation, Montgomery. You traded with the Injuns for hostages—that right?"

"Used to work along that line. The Army isn't paying for hostages any longer. I'm thinking about heading south."

Clue took out his timepiece and then stared off down the road. "I wonder if Mack has run into trouble. It ain't like him to run late on this spur. He knows that supper is at six."

"Do you mean the stage?"

"Yep. It usually rolls in about this time. If you want to see the lady off safely, it pulls out again at sunup. We've sleeping quarters for sixteen visitors. You're welcome to spend the night and take your meals with us."

"I appreciate that, Clue. I'll see what she has in mind."

"It ain't none of my affair, but that gal appears to have been a hostage herself. You wouldn't be running from the Owatawna?"

Kit didn't bother lying to him, but he felt that Deana's suffering was no one's business. Some people assumed that any woman taken by the Indians was automatically defiled.

"There was a wagon train about forty miles

southeast of here. She was the only survivor of an attack by Iron Claw. She escaped the Indians, but had a rough time until I found her. Her clothes were badly damaged in the raid, so I lent her my spare set."

Clue looked as if he didn't quite believe Kit, but he let the matter drop. He again peered down the road and looked at his watch.

"Nope, it ain't like Mack to be late for chow."

"How many guns are on the place?" Kit asked. "In case there's trouble."

"If you mean people who can shoot, there's only myself, Skeet—the boss of this here station—and a couple of men who trade off as driver and guard, Andy and Neal. A young Mexican named Manuel works here too, but I don't know if he can shoot."

"That's not much of a defense against Puma," Kit said.

"There's an escort with the stage—provided they get here."

Kit looked down the route the stage would take. He thought he could detect a minute column of dust, but it was quickly gone. If Mack and the soldiers were coming, they were still a couple of miles away.

"Chow's on!" someone called from the two-story house.

"Let's go eat, son," Clue suggested. "We can worry just as well on a full stomach."

Kit entered the dining room, which had two long tables and benches for seating up to twenty people. Kit took a place at the end, so he'd be able to watch the door and look out the main window. He recognized Skeet Tellar and his wife from their visits to the fort. Both were in their late thirties, and they had a daughter, Priscilla, about ten years old.

Jeff and Deana entered the room together. She was wearing a dress and had brushed out her hair. Except for a bruise on her face and scratches on her exposed arms, she looked radiant. Kit was amazed at how attractive he found her. Deana was quite beautiful!

As was customary when a lady entered, all the men rose to their feet. Deana seemed somewhat embarrassed by the courtesy, but took a place across from Kit. She paused to be introduced to each of the men at the table. Jeff casually took a seat right next to her.

Mrs. Teller and Priscilla brought a plate of bread and a large pan of stew to each table. There was water, lemonade, or coffee to drink.

"I hardly recognized you," Kit told Deana. "When you walked into the room, I thought you must be an actress. You look pretty enough to be onstage."

Deana smiled, blushing noticeably at the compliment. "It feels good to be cleaned up and wearing decent clothing again."

Jeff laughed, preventing Kit from continuing the conversation. "I thought you were something special, Deana, even in Kit's ragged attire."

"I think there is something wrong with your eyesight, Jeff," she said, laughing lightly. "Maybe you've gotten too much sun while out riding herd on those cattle of yours."

"If I'm dazzled, it has nothing to do with the sun," he said, as smooth as silk. "A lady like you blinds a man to everything else."

Kit was disgusted. Jeff surely knew how to butter up Deana—and he could spread it on thick!

"What are your plans, little lady?" Clue asked. "Are you going to take the stage back to civilization?"

Kit noticed that she glanced at him before speaking. Then she gave Clue a smile. "I haven't decided what to do yet. I suppose I'll have to make some plans."

"She's got a place with us," Jeff announced. "We can use someone to help with the chores—at least until my sister has the baby. It'll be quite a while before she can do housework again. That would give you a home and time to plan for the future."

The gleam in Jeff's eyes made it obvious that he wanted Deana—but not as a housekeeper for the family.

Kit chewed hard on a forkful of stew, trying to keep his temper under control. He told himself that he had no right to decide anything about Deana's future. She was a grown woman, able to make up her own mind. But if she couldn't see through Jeff's facade, she wasn't very bright!

"What do you think, Kit?" Deana asked him. "What would you do, if you were me?"

"What would I do?" he asked in a voice that actually squeaked.

"You saved my life." Deana's voice was as soft and tranquil as a quiet summer evening. "I have a deep respect for your opinion."

He looked up to meet her eyes. Again her expression puzzled him.

"I. . . ." He cleared his throat, feeling warm and uncomfortable. "I think that. . . ."

Jeff chuckled. "Kit's a man of action, not words. You can't expect someone like him to know how a lady thinks or feels."

Neal joined in to make fun of Kit. "From what I've heard, Kit is a loner, a man with ice in his veins and a lump of granite for a heart.

Who else could deal with Iron Claw and live to tell about it?"

"He's got either raw courage or no brains," Andy joked. "It takes a special kind of man to deal with the Owatawna."

Kit had no idea how the conversation had taken such a turn. He had been minding his own business, not saying anything to anybody—then, bang! Suddenly he was the butt of everyone's jokes. He saw Jeff laughing and having a good time. If Deana hadn't been present, he'd have pushed Jeff's face into his bowl of stew.

But Kit didn't have to squirm under the heckling very long. The door flew open and banged against the inside wall. A Mexican boy, out of breath and flushed with excitement, rushed inside.

"The stage is coming fast!" he panted. "There's only one trooper riding with it!"

Kit was outside before the stage jerked to a halt in the yard. The driver jammed on the brake and jumped down. The guard was slumped over the driver's seat. Blood on his shirt and glazed, staring eyes showed he was dead.

The lone soldier was doubled over his saddle. Kit went over to help him down. "Roaker!" Kit exclaimed.

The sergeant fell into his arms, but then managed to get his feet under him. He looked at Kit with a haggard, fearful expression.

"Iron Claw!" he gasped. "He hit us at the stream crossing. We . . . we had just picked up Al Squash and Kelly. We didn't have a chance. They cut us to pieces."

Kit put an arm around the soldier to support him just as Al and Kelly got out of the stage. The other man inside was dead.

"This is all your fault, Montgomery!" Al declared. "You were the one who sent those bloodthirsty Indians after us!"

Kit didn't reply, as he was helping Roaker into the house.

Mrs. Tellar quickly cleared one of the tables. "Put him down here," she directed Kit. "Priscilla, get me some hot water and the bandages out of the storeroom."

Deana helped Roaker get his shirt off. The wound had bled some, but the bullet had gone clear through his shoulder. If no bones or arteries were damaged, he would have a good chance of pulling through.

Kit didn't wait to see about him, for he had other pressing matters to attend to. He went out and helped unharness the team. There was no time to get a fresh team into the traces, for riders had appeared off in the distance.

"Yonder they are!" Clue shouted. "We can't get away by stage."

"Take a good look, Montgomery," Squash sneered. "Iron Claw and his whole tribe are out there!"

Kit paused to take inventory of the war party. Iron Claw's paint horse was out in front of about twenty-five other mounted warriors, and most of them had rifles.

"And look thataway!" Neal shouted. "There are others coming too."

At the upper end of the valley were at least a dozen more Indians, fanned out in a skirmish line. One of them was Puma.

"Let's break out the ammunition," Clue said solemnly. "It's going to be raining lead right soon."

They shoved the stagecoach off to one side of the yard, then hustled the horses into the barn. Neal and Manuel took up positions to defend that building. Andy and the driver used the stage for cover, while Kit, Al, Kelly, Jeff, and Skeet found firing positions inside the inn. Clue was behind the watering trough, between the stagecoach and the barn.

The way station was too large to protect with such a small force. The back of it was exposed to attack, as were all sides. There were only ten of them—eleven if Roaker was able to shoot—against a small army of well-trained men.

Iron Claw rode around the front of the fortified station, careful to stay out of range. Puma came from the other way until the two war parties met. After a parley, a lone brave tied a white cloth to a lance and rode toward the armed men. Kit recognized Two Hands, one of Iron Claw's best men.

"Iron Claw say this," he called, stopping his horse in the yard. "You give us man called Al Squash and his friend. They kill our people. They must pay."

"And if we don't?" Skeet asked.

"We kill all of you."

A gun blast filled the room, ending the talk. Kit spun on Al and saw the man's smoking pistol.

"There's your answer, you red scum!" Al bellowed, cocking his gun to fire again.

Two Hands had been nicked along the ribs. He spun the horse around and bolted from the yard. Al didn't have time to get off a second shot.

"You ain't got the brains of a toad," Skeet told him in disgust. "As long as we could keep them Indians talking, they weren't killing anyone. The Army will come looking for the stage and escort in two or three days."

Al grunted with contempt. "I didn't want none of you thinking too hard about that offer. You might have decided to take them up on it."

"It's tempting," Skeet admitted. "You stirred up this whole affair by killing some helpless Owatawna. Now you've got a wagon train massacred and nine more men killed. I don't want to add my wife and daughter to the list of people who've paid for your crime."

"Listen to him!" Al said with disgust. "Since when has it been a crime to kill Indians?"

Jeff moved over to where Deana and Mrs. Tellar were cleaning the sergeant's wound. Kit couldn't help noticing how Jeff put a consoling hand on Deana's shoulder. He said something, and she gave him a tight smile before looking over at Kit. When her eyes met his, a knot twisted inside Kit, a knot that he couldn't untangle. What unknown power was upsetting him so?

"The Indians seem to be discussing their course of action again," Skeet observed. "I hope you didn't intend to kill that warrior, Squash. I'd hate to think you were that bad a shot."

Al snorted. "I only wanted to send them a message. It ain't proper to kill a man under the flag of truce—even a stinking Indian."

"That's really funny," Kit retorted. "You killed women and children who were totally defenseless, and now you uphold the code of honor about a white flag. You're either a hypocrite or an idiot."

Al's face turned dark with anger. "When this is over, Montgomery, it'll be just the two of us—you and me!"

"Iron Claw isn't likely to give us the chance to fight among ourselves, Squash. He's got plenty of men and ammunition for all of us."

"Yeah, and I noticed that Puma came in from the other direction. That tells me something too, Montgomery," Al said.

"What?" Kit demanded.

"You've got a woman he wants. I bet she came from that wagon train and you traded our lives for hers!"

"Too bad Iron Claw didn't get the job done."

Al guffawed. "That's right, it's too bad. Then you'd only have to fight Puma—for the same squaw!"

Kit turned from the window, pointed his gun right at Al, and cocked the hammer. The man gaped with surprise. He was looking at death—and knew it.

"You ever call Miss Shaw anything but a lady again, Squash, and I'll kill you." Kit's grim expression was proof that this wasn't an idle threat.

The man's face drained of color, leaving it ashen. He tried to muster some bravado, working a smile onto his lips. "I hear you, Montgomery. We're all in this together. No need to fight among ourselves."

"They're up to something," Skeet said excitedly.

"They're breaking into small groups," Kelly said, watching from his post at the window. "I think we should pull everyone inside the house. Big as it is, we'll have a hard time defending it."

"It wasn't built as a fort," Skeet agreed. "It has windows on all sides and a door at the rear. The upper story has a ledge and windows too. That's a lot of openings to cover, and it's all wood. If they decide to burn us out, we won't have a prayer."

"We'll worry about the downstairs for the time being," Kit advised. "If they surround us, we'll split up and watch all sides."

"Ammunition will be our main concern," Skeet told him. "I doubt that we've got more than two hundred rounds."

Kit took a quick inventory. "I have about thirty."

"I've got less than twenty," Jeff called out.

"About the same for me and Al," Kelly said. "We've been doing battle with them devils for twenty-four hours already."

"Any extra on the stage?" Kit asked.

"Maybe a box of shotgun shells," Roaker told him. "We shot about everything we had to get away. I've got maybe a dozen rounds for my carbine and whatever is in my handgun."

"We'll have to be careful with our shots. No need throwing lead at everything that moves. Wait until you have a target," Kit said.

"With Owatawna?" Kelly was not optimistic. "They don't offer themselves as targets, Montgomery."

"Then wait until one of them is about to scalp you. At least make sure that you've got a chance of hitting something."

Deana moved over to Kit and gently rested her hand on his arm. When he glanced at her, he could see the inner terror that gripped her.

"Remember your promise, Kit," she said quietly.

"I won't let them take you," he said firmly. "Puma will never lay a hand on you."

She rewarded him with a nervous smile. "Thank you. I needed to hear you say it again."

Kit watched her move back over to huddle with Mrs. Tellar and Priscilla. Once the attack came, they could help load rifles. Until then, they had to sit back and wait.

Turning back to his window, Kit was filled with a new determination. The girl had suffered enough. If he had to, he'd slip out and find Puma in the dark. He'd kill him any way he could, making sure Deana would never have to endure his touch. But he knew it was an empty vow, for there were no certainties in a game of death.

Chapter Eleven

They came like dust devils swirling in the wind, dark blotches against the bright setting sun. They darted past on horseback, scarcely visible beneath the necks or stomachs of their horses. The firing was rapid and deadly, but few bullets found a mark.

The windows of the house were soon shattered by bullets. Beneath the stagecoach, Andy cried out in surprise and fell onto his face. Kit risked a quick look at him, but was too far away to make out any signs of life.

As guns blasted away throughout the house, the rooms filled with acrid smoke. Three horses had been shot down in the yard, but only one Indian had been hit, and even he crawled away during the gunfire. Iron Claw's men were well trained and made few mistakes in the attack.

The battle raged for over an hour. The Indi-

113

ans took up positions in the brush and nearby ditches, and kept a steady assault on the main house. As dusk approached, the attack was broken off. The Indians retreated out of rifle range and gathered in small groups.

Manuel helped Neal over to the house. Gray from shock, he'd been hit in the chest and was breathing in ragged gasps. There was nothing to be done for him.

"In the dark, we can't hold the barn," the young Mexican said.

"They were counting the guns," Kit told the others. "They know our strength now. Next they'll hit our weakest point."

"That would be the barn," Skeet declared. "Manuel is right. We can't hold it."

"Get everyone into the house. We'll make a plan for defending the station," Kit said.

Clue came in to join them. When asked about Andy, he shook his head. "They tagged him several times after he went down. Hard to say which shot killed him."

"How about the driver?"

"He's hit too hard to move. I don't reckon he's got more than an hour. We didn't do worth a hoot against those braves this first round."

"Near as I could tell, we hit only three or four. There aren't any bodies out there." Kelly took a deep breath and paused. "Things don't look good."

"Here comes another Indian with a white flag," Al announced. "They must not have gotten our message last time."

Kit looked past Al and saw Iron Claw on his paint horse.

"He'll want to speak to me," Kit said. "If you try to shoot him, Squash, you won't have to wait for them to kill you—I'll shoot you myself."

"Whatever you say, Montgomery," Al said, grinning wickedly. "After all, he's your pal. You go out there and have a nice chat."

Kit left his rifle inside the house and walked out to meet the chief of the Owatawna. He knew it was a waste of time to talk, but what options were open to him?

Iron Claw sat his horse proudly, his painted face a mask of total control. He looked at the way station and then back at Kit.

"I want the two trappers, Soldier Kit. Give me those men, and you will not die by my hand."

Kit faced the chief squarely. "I agree with you that Squash and Kelly deserve to die for killing your people in cold blood. They should hang for murder. But your people have killed many others in cold blood. There can be no justice in killing innocent people."

"White men are not punished for killing Indians. You have told me this."

"That's right. But Squash won't go unpunished for his crimes. I will see that the Army tries him for bringing about the deaths of those you have killed here and in the wagon train. He is the reason for the bloodshed. He would have us all at war."

"We are at war," Iron Claw said. "There can be no peace."

"And you cannot win against the Army. They will hunt you down and kill you and your followers. They will put your women and children on reservations. It will be the end of your freedom."

"I do not want your blood on my hands, Soldier Kit. Send me the two trappers."

"I can't do that, Iron Claw. It is not our way."

The chief nodded. "So it will be, Soldier Kit. I offer the white squaw life. If she comes now, Puma will see that she is not harmed."

"You know her answer to that," Kit said.

"She prefers death," Iron Claw replied without hesitation.

Kit watched the chief ride away. The Indian would have a clear conscience, for he had offered Kit a chance to live, though Puma still wanted him dead.

Once Kit got back in the house, everyone gathered to discuss their limited choices.

"It's twenty miles to my father's ranch," Jeff said. "After dark, we might be able to get through their lines."

"Even if we made it, there aren't enough men at your place to do much good against Puma and Iron Claw," Kit replied.

"It's seventy-five miles to the fort," Skeet told him. "The next way station is forty miles away and has only a couple of retired soldiers working there."

"And by the time anyone could reach the fort and return, we'd long since be dead." Kelly shook his head. "No matter how you slice it, Iron Claw and Puma still end up eating the whole cake."

Roaker sat up and gingerly tested his shoulder. "He's right about that, Montgomery. The stagecoach patrol should have made it back to the fort by tomorrow night or the following day. By the time the Army sends a detachment, it will be all over for us. I don't see any way out."

Kit was thinking hard. "Once the horses are gone, we'll be stuck here. We shouldn't let that happen."

"I don't like the idea of being trapped on foot any more than you do," Jeff said. "But what can we do about it?"

"They're sure to fire the barn," Kelly pointed out.

"So what's the answer, Indian lover?" Squash jeered. "How do we defend the barn in the dark? Them Owatawna will come to get the horses and burn the place down."

"There are two teams and a few horses," Kit said, thinking aloud. "We could hitch up the stage and another large wagon, and make a break for it. A fresh team can run twenty miles. If those Indian ponies are a little tuckered out, they might not keep up."

"But what about the other team?" Skeet asked. "They've done a full day's work. They wouldn't last two miles."

"The wagon would run behind the coach. Several men with rifles might be able to keep the Indians off the lead group. I'm not saying it wouldn't get some of us killed, but right now we all stand to die. The wagon could cover the stage during the escape."

"That's a thought," Clue agreed. "We could put the ladies and Priscilla in the coach. Roaker can ride well enough to act as guard. Skeet could drive, since he's the only married man among us and has the most experience with a team."

"Whoa!" Al Squash didn't like the way the plan was shaping up. "That means that the rest of us would be killed. I ain't volunteering for something like that."

"We'd have a couple of horses tied to the wagon," Kit continued. "Once the team had run themselves out and the Indians got too close, we'd abandon the wagon and ride the saddled horses."

"I've got to hand it to you, Montgomery," Skeet said. "Your plan ain't perfect, but it does give some of us a slim chance."

"A few problems are still facing us," Kelly said from his post by the window.

"Such as?" Skeet asked.

"They might set fire to the barn tonight. No team could manage that rough road in the dark, so we'll have to protect the barn and the animals through the night."

"We could all move into the barn to defend it," Manuel suggested.

"That would make our intentions obvious, and they could kill us all by setting fire to it," Kit pointed out.

"What other choice do we have, Montgomery?" Skeet asked wearily. "We haven't the manpower to hold both the house and barn once it's dark."

"I don't think we have any other choice. We have to split our forces. Four men might be able to hold the barn, while Roaker and the others hold the house."

"And if the Indians set fire to the barn?" Al asked, still not happy with any of the ideas.

"Then those in here would cover the others while they ran from the barn to the house."

Clue shrugged. "Makes no difference after that anyhow. If they torch the barn, we have no plan of escape. Once we're on foot, the battle is over and they've got us."

"We'll move the coach inside the barn," Kit said. "Sometime before daylight, we'll hitch up both teams and saddle the horses."

"I don't like it," Al grumbled. "Whatever we do, we're bound to lose."

"The way I see it, you've already lost, Al," Kit said. "If we get out of this, I'll see you before a military tribunal. And then I'll do my best to see that you get what's coming to you."

Al laughed gruffly. "Don't count on it, soldier boy. Even if we do get out of this, you're as good as dead."

"Who's going out to the barn?" Skeet asked, ignoring the exchange of threats.

"Not me," Al said. "It'll be certain death."

"Let's draw straws," Manuel suggested. "Four short and three long."

Mrs. Tellar pulled some straws from her broom and handed them to Roaker. He broke seven straws into the desired lengths and then tucked them into his good hand. He held them out to the others.

"Who's first?"

Kit moved over and drew a short straw. "All right, I'm one. Who else is going out to the barn?"

The others drew from Roaker's hand. Clue and Manuel both ended up with short straws. The last two were for Al and Kelly. But Al refused to draw.

"I'm not going out there to be killed. If the rest of you want to die, go right ahead."

Kelly took both straws and tossed the long one at Al. "All right, Squash. I'll go play hide and seek with the Indians. You sit here and cower behind the women."

Al's face grew red, but for once he had nothing to say.

"Help me to the door," Roaker said. "I can see the yard and barn from there. We'll give you what cover we can."

The ammunition was quickly divided, and Mrs. Tellar took possession of the shotgun. Then the men went out to move the wagon into the barn. The Indians saw them but didn't attack. From their point of view, the trapped people could do nothing with an empty, horseless coach.

It was dark when the four men entered the barn. Kit would have liked a word with Deana, but there was no time for talk. The only thing he minded about drawing a position in the barn was that it separated him from her—and it left Jeff inside the house to hold her hand.

"Twenty rounds of ammunition won't last very long," Kelly observed. "How good are you with a knife, Manuel?"

Manuel's eyes grew wide with fear. "Knife?"

"Don't let him scare you," Clue told Manuel. "Be careful to conserve your shots, and it won't come to hand-to-hand combat."

"Two doors and a loft," Kit said after looking over the inside of the barn. "A dozen horses to keep calm, and forty warriors out to scalp us."

"How are we supposed to keep them out?" Clue wanted to know. "You got a plan for that, Montgomery?"

"Let's nail the rear door shut. With it sealed and blocked, one man can hold it. We'll worry about protecting the front and the loft."

"That leaves one man in the loft and two at

the other door," Kelly said. "Where do you want me?"

"Clue can take the back door, Manuel the loft. You and I will hold the main doors."

They boarded up the rear door and piled lumber and wagon parts against the braces, leaving plenty of openings for Clue to shoot through. Then Manuel went to the loft, and Kelly and Kit took up a position at the main doors.

"What are you going to do when this is all over, Montgomery?" Kelly asked to pass the time.

"I hadn't given it much thought. First off, I'd like to live through the night."

"That won't be easy. If they decide to burn us out, this war is lost."

"If we see them start a fire, we'd better hitch up the teams. Our only chance will be a mad dash in the dark."

"Out on that rough, winding road?" Kelly laughed at the thought. "We'd be turned over and busted into splinters in five minutes."

"I'm open to any other ideas."

"Sorry, Montgomery. I'm fresh out."

Kit watched the shadows outside beginning to move in on them. It wouldn't be long now. Iron Claw and Puma were in the dark somewhere, masterminding the attack. Their first raid had been to feel out the strength of those in the way station. Now they were ready to move in for the kill.

Chapter Twelve

Kit burrowed in between the heavy sacks of grain. Two hefty bales of gunnysacks were stacked in front of him, with only a small crack in the door for his rifle. He was as well protected as anyone could be, under the circumstances. Kelly was on the other side of the door, hunched behind the forge and watering trough. Manuel and Clue were also in position. Now it was just the four of them—against forty warriors.

"They're starting to move," Kelly observed. "They know our strength now. This will be a deliberate attack, aimed at one place at a time."

"If we can hold on till daylight, we can still survive this battle," Kit said. "All we need is some luck."

Kelly shouldered his rifle and watched for a target. "I don't mind telling you, Montgomery, I'd rather have you at my side than Al. He looks out only for himself."

Kit glanced over at him. "Too bad you didn't part company with him before killing those Owatawna."

Kelly sighed regretfully. "What can I say, Montgomery? A man don't think straight when he's got a gut full of whiskey."

"That's no excuse, Kelly. Only a fool drinks himself into trouble."

"I know that now," Kelly replied. "Too bad I probably won't get the chance to mend my ways."

"The Indians are heading toward us," Kit said, movement outside catching his eye. "Iron Claw can smell victory."

A blast filled the room as Kelly fired. He jacked another shell into the chamber and chuckled. "There's one who won't be celebrating."

Kit might have praised his shooting, but there wasn't time. The Owatawna were attacking.

Shots were fired from both the barn and the house. Though every man knew he had to make his bullets count, most rounds missed their mark. The Indians used the cover well, returning fire and moving closer.

Kit caught one man in his sights and fired—

a miss. The man had moved to another hiding place just as Kit had pulled the trigger. He cocked the rifle again and searched for a clear shot.

Debris from the door clouded his vision as several Indians returned fire. He blinked at the dust and specks, trying to watch for a target.

"Coming in!" Kelly cried over the roar of the gunfire.

Kit turned toward the loft, searching for Manuel. Two Indians were climbing down the ladder, having evidently scaled the barn and entered the loft from above. Manuel was probably dead.

Kit fired carefully, knocking the first Indian off the ladder. The second jumped onto Kelly. The trapper met him, but lost his rifle in the process. Kelly pulled his big skinning knife, and the two disappeared into the darkness of the room.

Kit couldn't take time to help. Indians were storming the doorway. He fired at the group of three that appeared. The guns from the house also were blasting away. Two Indians went down, but the third launched himself over the barricade at Kit.

It was impossible to get off another shot, so Kit used the rifle as a club to block the flying body. The Indian slammed into him and the rifle and knocked him over. He landed on his back with the man on top of him.

Kit squirmed, trying to roll the man off. The Indian put a knee into his stomach, knocking the wind from his lungs. He drove a knife downward at Kit, but it missed the mark. Kit struck back with his fist and caught the Indian on the side of the face. The blow was solid enough to roll him over. Kit scrambled to get on top of him, but a second Indian appeared, diving over the pile of sacks at him. There was no time to finish off the first. Kit ducked low, hitting the second one at his ankles and upending him on top of the first Indian.

With his rifle lost on the straw-covered floor, Kit drew his handgun from its holster. He fired point-blank into the two Indians. It took three shots to hit them both, then a fourth to make sure they were done for. With no chance to catch his breath, he looked around for his rifle.

Kelly had beaten his man. He had blood running from a slash on his arm, but he was back at his position with his rifle.

Three bodies lay outside near the doorway. Roaker and the others in the house were doing their best to help defend the barn. The firing was heavy and constant. The wooden doors were punched full of holes, and lead pellets screamed off the walls and the brick foundation of the forge.

"They must need horses," Kelly said, during a short lull in the shooting. "Otherwise they would have set fire to the place."

"They might also think the stage or wagons have ammunition in them. Could be that they don't have any more ammo than we do."

"Manuel didn't last long in the loft. We might have more of them coming in that way."

"Can you see Clue?" Kit asked.

"Too dark. I thought I heard a few shots from back there. I hope he's still with us."

The stalls were full of horses. At least two of them had been felled by stray bullets. That wouldn't help their chances. The stage needed eight horses. That wouldn't leave many to pull the other wagon. When it came to riding stock, they had had only five to start with.

The shooting became more sporadic, and a few of the Indians pulled back from the attack. They hadn't fared well against the barn or the house. Taking either would require a new strategy.

"They'll come at us with fire next time," Kelly said. "This kind of fight cost them too many braves."

"That will put an end to us. I think we've got to risk getting the stage and wagon hitched up. When the barn catches fire, we'll break for the road."

"We might get lucky, if they don't expect it. Maybe they won't be able to get their own horses for a few minutes. That would give us time to cross the worst of the trail. Once out into the open, we could give them a run for their money."

"Let's see about getting some help out here. They've pulled back for the moment."

"I'll slip over to the house," Kelly volunteered. "You can get Clue and start moving the animals into position. It won't be easy, since this barn wasn't meant to hold two teams in harness at the same time."

Kit took a last look and then hurried toward the back of the barn. Clue was still alive, although he'd been nicked by one bullet and had splinters in one hand from another.

"Help me get the fresh team up to the stage. We're getting out of here pretty soon."

"Can't be none too soon for me, son. I thought them devils was coming right through the walls for a time. I don't know how many I killed, but I hit at least two or three."

"Sort out the horses. I'll go up and check on Manuel. I'm afraid they got him."

"Too bad," Clue said quietly. "He was a good boy."

Kit climbed up into the loft, drawing his handgun in case more Indians had slipped into the open window. There didn't seem to be any danger, so he searched until he found the young Mexican. He was dead.

Moving to look out the window, Kit felt regret and anguish fill his soul at the sight of the dead. There were no winners in war, only survivors.

Watching the yard for shadows, he could see no movement. Apparently the attack had been broken off for a while. He hoped that would give his group time enough to prepare for their mad dash for freedom. The odds of surviving such an attempt were not good, but better to risk it than let Iron Claw decide their fate. Once the Indian chief decided the loss of lives was too great, he would resort to fire and burn them out.

Kit backed away from the window and went down to help Clue. It was no later than midnight. No doubt the Indians were tired, but waiting until morning would not help them. Now that it was night, they could surround the place and wait. Once the barn and the house were burning, they would only have to pick off the fleeing people.

*   *   *

Deana held her breath as Kelly entered the house and ducked for cover. Mrs. Tellar quickly wrapped a crude bandage around his arm.

"What about the others?" Roaker was the first to ask the dreadful question.

"Manuel is out of it," Kelly replied. "The stage driver died before the first attack. I don't know about Clue. We heard some shooting from the back of the barn. I think he's still with us."

"What about Kit?" Deana could wait no longer.

Kelly grinned in her direction. "He's a cat, that one. I think he's got nine lives."

"Then . . . then he's all right?" she asked softly.

"So far. Was anyone hit in here?"

"I caught a slug in the leg, but it ain't too bad," Skeet told him. "Jeff got a face full of glass and is cut up some, but he can see to shoot."

"What do you want, Kelly?" Al asked with a growl. "If you're looking for men to go out and hold the barn, forget it."

"Kit and I agree that we have one chance left," Kelly said, ignoring his partner. "If the Indians come with fire, we'll have to make our move. He and Clue are hitching up the teams.

At the first sign of fire, we're going to make a break for the fort."

"In the dark?" Mrs. Tellar asked incredulously. "The first mile is all hills and winding road."

"We can hope they won't be able to pursue us right away. The wagon will follow the stagecoach and try to keep off the Indians until we hit open terrain. Then it would be a race."

"Are we going to draw straws again to see who goes on the stage?" Al demanded. "I ain't going to commit suicide by riding in that wagon."

Kelly glowered at Al. "You'll ride next to me—in the wagon. If we make it to open ground, we'll switch to the horses."

"Since when are you giving me orders?"

Kelly faced him squarely. "Since right now, Squash. We need your gun, but don't press your luck. If necessary, I'll break one of your legs and throw you in that wagon. You'd have to fight that way."

Al rose to his feet. He'd never tested his strength against Kelly, for he'd always been the boss. It was a shock to have the man standing up to him.

"You need some help?" Skeet asked Kelly, to break the chill between the two men.

"Someone who can help harness the ani-

mals. I don't know the first thing about it,"
Kelly replied, still glaring at Al.

"I'll get out there," Skeet said.

"All right." Kelly turned to the others. "The
rest of you get ready to leave. Hold your positions at the windows until the word is given.
Then we'll have to load into the stage and the
wagon, and get going."

Deana looked past Skeet as he opened the
door and hurried across to the barn. She
wished she could go with him. She had felt secure with Kit, believing that somehow he'd
manage to fulfill his promise not to let the Indians ever take her again.

"Are you all right?" Jeff asked, coming to
stand at her side.

"Yes."

"Don't worry, Deana. We'll get out of this."

The words sounded sincere, but Jeff wasn't
Kit. When Kit told her everything would be
all right, she believed him, no matter what
challenge faced them.

Chapter Thirteen

The first sign was the distant glow of three separate fires. Then the black sky was streaked with the yellow trails of fire arrows.

The roof of the barn smoldered and then broke into flames. Soon the house was also on fire—ample incentive to try the daring escape plan.

Skeet drove the stagecoach out first, stopping at the door of the house. Everyone piled out at once, while Clue brought up the wagon. Kit secured four saddle horses to the wagon, as Al, Kelly, and Jeff climbed into it. Roaker and the women got into the stage.

Shots rang out, but the teams quickly headed out of the yard. Even as the stagecoach and the wagon bolted down the road, Kit could see the Indians running for their own mounts.

Skeet and Clue ran the teams, risking a devastating wreck on every curve. The Indians began the chase a hundred yards behind them, but the Indian riders closed the distance quickly. Though Kit and the others in the wagon fired at the pursuing shadows, their aim was spoiled by the bouncing of the wagon. In a matter of moments, the Owatawna were only fifty feet behind them.

"This is crazy!" Al cried. "We ain't got no chance in this wagon!"

"We've got to keep them off the stage until we hit the open ground," Kit said. "It's only another half mile or so."

But Al wasn't listening to Kit. He jerked loose the reins of a horse and jumped to its back. He spurred the mount and left the wagon behind.

Kit and Kelly kept firing at the pursuing Indians, but it was impossible to hit anything, since the Owatawna rode too low on their horses. It was only a matter of seconds before they would overtake the wagon.

"We ain't going to make it!" Jeff shouted. "Let's take the horses and try to protect the stage."

Kit fired once more and then found that Clue had slumped forward on the seat of the wagon. He turned and grabbed the reins, trying to keep the team on the winding, uneven road. Kelly and Jeff both abandoned the wagon, the warriors right behind them.

As Kit tried to hold Clue up and drive the team, an Indian jumped into the back of the wagon bed. Kit didn't have time to grab for his horse, since the brave tried to club him with a tomahawk.

Rolling over, Kit threw himself against the Indian. The two of them fell into the wagon bed as the horses left the road. The bouncing of the wagon tossed the men about. The wagon veered to the side as the team avoided a tree and went into a gully.

Kit felt the wagon turning over. He pushed off from the wood floor, diving in the opposite direction. The wagon flipped over on both Clue and the Indian as Kit slammed into the side of a hill and somersaulted into the bottom of the wash.

The world spun before Kit's eyes, and he had the wind knocked out of him. Before he could recover, two braves were on him.

Something crashed into the side of his head, and Kit lost all sensation. His mind managed a last fleeting image of a young woman—Deana.

Deana looked out the window of the stagecoach, but she could no longer see the wagon behind them. Al, Kelly, and Jeff were riding alongside. But where was Kit? What had happened to him?

She called out to Kelly, but he couldn't hear her. Some of the Indians had gone after the wagon, so there were not as many in pursuit; however, the Indians were gaining on them. Though the flatlands were only a few rough turns away, the Owatawna had formed a crude circle around the stage. The escape plan had failed.

Mrs. Tellar and Priscilla were huddled on the floor. Deana still sat on the bouncing seat, looking back for Kit. She was holding the shotgun but had been unable to reload it in the dark.

Skeet kept the team moving while Roaker continued to shoot at the warriors, but the situation was hopeless. Al's horse stumbled from being shot, so he was forced to swerve over and jump onto the stage. He climbed inside with Deana and began to shoot out the window.

"What happened to Kit?" she shouted.

"He's gone!" Al yelled back at her. "They got him."

Deana's heart constricted painfully. She held on to the door and rocked with the stage, but she refused to believe the words. She shook her head, then grabbed Al's arm.

"Did you see it? How do you know he's dead?"

Al jerked away from her and fumbled to reload his handgun. "He went down with the wagon. He didn't have a chance to get to his horse. He's dead, I tell you!"

Deana fell back, tears flooding her eyes. As long as Kit was alive, there had been hope. Now there was no hope for any of them. Puma would overtake the stage. He would make her his bride, and she would spend the rest of her life in shame and degradation.

Suddenly the wagon lurched and slid. The wagon wheels locked as Skeet threw his weight against the brake. Deana found herself on the floor with Mrs. Tellar and Priscilla.

"They shot one of the team!" Al cried. "They've got us now!"

As the stagecoach came to a jerky halt, Kelly and Jeff dismounted and dropped down to take cover under it. Roaker had passed out during the pounding ride atop the coach, pinning Skeet to the driver's seat. The Indians formed a wide circle around the coach and held their position.

"Hear me, white dogs!" Puma called out. "Do you want to save your lives?"

"We're listening!" Al shouted back. "What's the deal?"

"I want the white woman," Puma called. "Give her to me, and you can have your lives. If you refuse, you will all die—and I will have her all the same."

Deana sat up straight. She preferred death to marrying Puma. But she had to consider the others, who were being offered a chance to live.

"No!" Skeet said. "You stay where you are, little lady. We ain't done yet."

"That's right," Jeff echoed. "We'll make them pay for our hides."

But Al turned and looked at her with wild eyes. He turned his gun toward her menacingly.

"You can save our lives, woman. We're all dead, unless you go out there. Think of the little girl. Think of all of us!"

Deana tried to muster her courage. She wanted to be brave and sacrifice herself for the others, but it was terribly difficult. She had seen Puma's hateful sneer. She knew he would treat her more like a captive animal than a person.

"What kind of man are you?" Mrs. Tellar asked Al furiously. "How can you even think of sending this poor girl out to that blood-thirsty savage?"

"He's right," Deana said softly. "You and

your daughter have a right to live. I can't be responsible for your deaths."

"*He's* the one responsible!" Mrs. Tellar retorted, pointing to Al. "He started this whole thing by killing those Owatawna. He's the one they should be after!"

But Deana had made up her mind. She moved over to the door and opened it.

"She's coming!" Al shouted. "You hear me, Puma? Keep your word. She's coming out right now!"

Deana stepped down from the coach and hesitated. Jeff and Kelly were only a few feet away. Jeff shook his head sorrowfully, but he was obviously afraid. None of them wanted to die.

Taking a deep breath, she began to walk into the dark. Within fifty feet, she was surrounded by three Indians. They led her up a nearby hill to where Puma was standing.

"You said the others could go free," she reminded him. "You promised."

He laughed contemptuously. "A promise to a white man is no promise. I should kill them, now that you are safe among us."

"Are you a man without honor? Does your word mean nothing?"

Puma scowled at her, then gestured to his braves. He grabbed her wrist and jerked her up next to him. Deana held her breath, repulsed at being drawn so close.

"You are mine, white woman. You will give me the power to defeat the soldiers."

She didn't know what he meant by that. He led her roughly to a horse and flung her onto its back. Then he swung up onto his own mount and gave an order in his native tongue. The warriors retreated from the stagecoach. He was keeping his word. He let the other passengers live.

Deana followed along quietly, trying to think of a way to escape or to kill herself. She knew the opportunity would present itself. One way or another, she would never be his bride.

Chapter Fourteen

The stage rolled into the fort and was greeted by Captain Yount. Roaker was in such bad shape that he couldn't give a report. Jeff had already taken his horses and headed for home. Skeet might have spoken up, but he was ashamed of what had happened. Taking his wife and daughter, he left to find them temporary housing. So only Al and Kelly remained to tell the story.

The captain paced the floor as Al told him how the Owatawna had attacked them on the trail and killed the escort—except for Roaker. He described the assault on the way station and the desperate escape in the dark. Deana's act of self-sacrifice he mentioned only briefly.

"What about Montgomery?" the captain asked.

"He never got to his horse," Kelly replied. "I saw him take the reins and try to help the old driver. We lost them in the dark, but I heard the wagon crash into the bottom of a wash. There were a dozen Indians on us right then. There's no way he could have gotten away."

Yount stood with his shoulders bowed. "Then it's war with the Owatawna. They've declared an all-out war against the whites."

"You're right about that," Al told him firmly. "The two men at the second way station came in with us. No stagecoach can run until this thing is taken care of."

"I'm expecting another company of men any day. When they arrive, we'll decide the best way to defeat Iron Claw. You say he has about forty warriors?"

"That's right."

Yount opened the door of his office for the two men. "I thank you for the report. Montgomery blamed you for killing that Owatawna family. If you started this war, you'll both end up facing charges."

"We only defended ourselves," Al said innocently. "Montgomery never did like us trappers. He told a pack of lies to put us in a bad light. We're only interested in keeping the peace, Captain. Ain't that right, Kelly?"

"That's right," Kelly finally said. "We don't

want any trouble with the Army or the Indians."

"So be it. You men are free to go—for the time being."

The two trappers walked out together, but stopped in the compound. Kelly looked hard at Al, no friendship remaining in his feelings for the man.

"This is where we part company, Squash. I never want to see your ugly puss again."

"What's with you, Kelly? Since when did you get so all-fired soft about Indians?"

Kelly caught hold of Al's shirtfront, jerked him forward, and shoved his face up next to Al's.

"You've got no conscience at all, you sagging bag of guts! Look at the number of people we got killed! A wagon train of innocent travelers, those soldiers, the guys on the stagecoach, and the others at the way station. It's our fault! We got them killed!"

Al seemed puzzled by Kelly's outburst. "I don't get you, Kelly. What's done is done. Them Indians might have gone on the warpath anyway. That Puma wants to kill every white in the country."

Kelly shook his own head in bewilderment. "It don't mean a thing to you, does it? You get twenty-five or thirty people killed, and you shrug it off. That pretty young gal gives up her life to save your miserable hide, and you don't even care what happens to her. Even Montgomery—it was his skill and daring that made our escape possible. You probably still hate his guts."

"What do you want from me, Kelly? It took all four of us to kill those six Owatawna. You ain't innocent—not by a long shot!"

Kelly shoved him away, furious at the man and at himself. Al had spoken the truth. Kelly had shot the old man during their drunken killing spree, so he was partly responsible for the many lives that had been lost.

He shoved his hands into his pockets and crossed the compound. He needed a drink—but he would never touch hard liquor again. Montgomery was right when he'd said that drinking was no excuse.

Kelly went into the trading post and sat at a table. He ordered one beer and sipped it slowly.

"Drinking alone?" Skeet was standing next to his table.

"I'm through drinking."

Skeet sat down in the chair opposite him, and ordered his own glass of beer. Then he remained silent for a time.

"What's on your mind?" Kelly knew the man wasn't there just to be sociable.

"I'm wondering about a few things, Kelly. I thought maybe you could clear them up for me."

"Such as?"

"Why did Iron Claw let us go?"

Kelly leaned back and rubbed the stubble on his chin. "Iron Claw was pursuing the wagon while Puma was after the stage. Something slowed Iron Claw down, and that allowed Puma to make a deal for the girl."

"Iron Claw wanted you and Al. What stopped him from following us and killing us all?"

"I don't know."

"Do you think Montgomery is dead?"

"He went into the gully with the wagon. That might be what held Iron Claw up. Maybe he put up a good fight."

"Is that what you think?"

"I don't know." Kelly was growing angry. "What do you want from me, Skeet? I don't know any more about Montgomery than you do. I saw the wagon go into the gully with him and Clue still on it. There was a crash, and that's all I know about it."

Skeet looked at his beer. "I can't help thinking about the girl. She gave her life for ours. That ain't going to be easy to live with."

"You're right about that," Kelly growled. "We never cared what happened to Deana Shaw, so long as we were all delivered to safety!"

Skeet took a long drink and set the glass down. "I tell myself that I had to think of my wife and daughter, Kelly. I tell myself that I had good reason for allowing that gal to go to that blasted savage. But I can't bear to look at my face in the mirror."

Kelly regarded the man with surprise. He had been feeling guilty, but he hadn't thought that Skeet would blame himself.

"You had to think of your wife and little girl. We all would have died if Puma hadn't made us that offer."

"Montgomery promised her that he wouldn't let Puma take her. He said that he would kill her first." Skeet lowered his head. "I didn't have the guts, Kelly. I put my rifle to my shoulder and aimed right at her back. I . . . I just couldn't pull the trigger."

Kelly put a hand on Skeet's shoulder. "Don't blame yourself, Skeet. The thought crossed my mind too, but I wanted to survive. There ain't a thing we can do about it now."

"After what we did, how do I face my child and wife, Kelly?"

"You make darn certain you treat your family as your most prized possession, Skeet. Deana gave you and your family a new lease on life. You'd do her a disservice not to make the most of it."

After a moment's thought, Skeet stood up and held out his hand to Kelly, who shook it. Skeet managed a brief smile as he said, "I never figured I'd ever thank a man like you for anything, Kelly. But I'm beholden to you for this talk. Thanks."

"Take care of those two gals of yours, Skeet. It's the only way to make Deana Shaw's sacrifice mean something."

Skeet tossed out a coin for the beer and left the room. Kelly watched him go, a knot forming in his stomach. A man's first concern had to be his family. Yet Skeet felt less than a man for allowing Deana to give herself up for capture.

With grim determination, Kelly rose from the table. He owed something to the girl, to Montgomery—and to himself. If it cost him his life, then so be it. Deana Shaw would not suffer at the hands of Puma—not if he could do anything about it.

Chapter Fifteen

I ron Claw glared at Puma. Both strong-willed, angry men, the two stood before the rest of the camp. Deana stood a few feet behind Puma, her wrists bound with rawhide straps. It had been a long, hard ride to the Indian encampment. She was tired, sore, and weak from lack of water or rest.

"What of the trappers?" Iron Claw demanded. "What of the men who murdered our sister and the others?"

Puma shrugged. "All whites will soon be gone from our land, my weak brother. I have the white squaw. I will have the power."

Iron Claw bridled. "You think that a white wife will make you strong enough to defeat their people, but you are a fool, Puma. A white woman is no different from an Indian woman. They have no magic, no power."

"You are wrong!" Puma cried. "Once it is

known that I have a white wife, warriors will come from all tribes to join us. They will know that we are the stronger force. We will drive away or kill all the whites in our country."

"You will only get more of our people killed. You do not think like a leader of Owatawna. You want only power and glory for yourself."

Puma's face grew dark with fury. "I will be war chief of all Owatawna, my brother. There is no one to stand against me. If you challenge me, I will kill you. I have the power. The warriors will follow me!"

Iron Claw looked directly at Deana and then back at Puma.

"The white woman is not yours, Puma. How can you have the power, when you can't even master your own woman?"

Puma frowned. "She is my captive. She will be my wife!"

But Iron Claw shook his head. "I have given her to another man, my brother. You have no claim to her."

Puma drew his knife and spun around, his eyes searching the warriors' faces. They backed away from him, seeing that he was ready to kill, to strike out at anyone.

"I see no challenger, my brother. I think you lie!"

Iron Claw nodded toward Two Hands. The

brave pulled back the tent flap on the guest hut. From its dark interior came a man Puma hated.

Kit was stiff and he had bruises on his leg and his forehead, but he was rested from a full night's sleep.

"Kit!" Deana cried. "Oh, Kit! You're alive!"

Puma turned and took a swipe at her with his knife. She backed away hastily, nearly falling down.

"This man claims the white woman. If you would have her, you must first defeat him in combat," Iron Claw said.

Wild with rage, Puma turned toward Kit. Obviously he wanted to destroy Kit, to be rid of him forever.

"I will cut out your heart, Soldier Kit," he vowed vehemently. "I will feed it to the dogs of our camp!"

Iron Claw tossed Kit a knife. Once Kit retrieved it, he faced Puma, and the entire camp gave them room to fight.

As Puma turned his knife, sunlight glistened and flashed on the blade. Kit knew the man would be quick, deadly, and utterly without mercy.

Circling warily, Kit favored his injured left leg although it didn't bother him. Showing a weakness might lull Puma into a mistake, so

Kit purposely limped and kept his weight on his right side.

The camp had been cleared, except for a smoldering fire pit. The two men moved away from it, each taking stock of the other. Kit waited, knowing Puma would bring the fight to him.

His free hand extended for balance, the Indian began making quick, short swipes with his blade, trying to slash Kit's face and body. He was the most deadly foe Kit had ever met in battle.

Kit avoided the blade of Puma's knife, and he countered with slashes of his own that came close but never made contact. Puma was very fast.

Kit shifted his weight to his left side and pretended that his knee was buckling. He backed away from Puma's desperate thrust and tried to ram his own blade home, but Puma batted it away with his knife.

Then Puma threw himself at Kit's legs, going into a roll. Kit tried to jump over him, but Puma threw up an arm and tripped him. Kit landed hard on his back and before he could get to his feet, the blade of Puma's knife came arching down at his throat. Kit instinctively blocked the thrust with his wrist and forearm, while trying to roll out from under the Indian.

Puma tried a second stab, trying to get by Kit's guard. Kit caught Puma's wrist in his left hand, driving his own blade up at the Indian. Puma caught hold of his wrist, and they rolled over twice, each straining against the strength of the other.

A sharp pain raced up Kit's shoulder as Puma's blade cut a two-inch gash. Kit dislodged him, tossing him off while rolling away to get back on his feet.

They circled once more, oblivious to the shouts of the spectators, the heat, and the dust that rose from their feet. Kit could feel the wetness from his bleeding shoulder. He wasn't badly hurt, but a few cuts would cost him blood and strength. Puma's skill was equal to or better than his own. He would have to use deception.

Kit staggered slightly, as if hurt worse than he actually was. He caught himself and continued to move. Puma's eyes searched for Kit's weaknesses, and he noticed the slight limp.

Shuffling away, Kit put his weight on his left leg and sank almost to his knee. It was the opening Puma had been waiting for. The man lunged forward, driving his knife hard and straight at Kit's chest—

The instant Puma committed himself, Kit jammed his left foot into the dirt and lunged in the opposite direction. He slashed upward, under Puma's guard, countering with a deadly thrust.

The Indian saw his error—too late. Kit's knife sank deep into the man's chest. He threw himself to the side, letting go of the knife handle.

Puma remained stooped over for a long moment. Then he rose to a standing position and examined the handle of the knife with confusion. Dropping his own knife into the dust, he put both hands on the handle and tried to pull the blade free. The force of that effort caused him to stagger several steps. He fell onto his face in the smoldering fire.

A couple of Indians hurried to pull him out of the hot coals, but Puma had suffered no pain from the burns. He was dead.

Kit was totally winded. It was all he could do to stand. Deana ran to him, tears streaming down her cheeks.

"I thought you'd been killed," she said, weeping against his shoulder. "They said that you didn't get off the wagon."

Breathing heavily, Kit put an arm around Deana. He didn't know what fate awaited them, for he'd just killed Iron Claw's brother.

The chief walked over and examined Puma. Then he came over to face Kit. He looked regretful, but his voice was clear and composed.

"I could have killed you, Soldier Kit. I let you live. Now you have killed my brother in battle. What shall I do with you?"

"Our lives are in your hands, Iron Claw. If the country is torn by war, we will probably all die in the fighting."

"I would have the fighting stop," the chief replied.

"If you are sincere, I'll take you to the fort to meet with the white chief. This fighting came about because white men killed your sister and several innocent people. I've told the white chief about it already. He doesn't want war. He'll listen to what you have to say."

Iron Claw gazed around at his people. There were new widows and orphans among them. He had lost good men during the fighting, and others were nursing injuries. A bitter war could end the Owatawna way of life. If he could gain a new peace, he might postpone the inevitable.

"I will ride to the fort with you, Soldier Kit. We will make peace."

Kelly was agape, unable to believe his eyes. Jeff Farley was also staring in disbelief. Kit had to smile at how stunned the two men looked. Kelly and Jeff carried rifles, and a spare horse trailed along behind them. When Kit, Deana, Iron Claw, and Two Hands met them face to face on the road, they were totally dumbfounded.

"I don't understand," Kelly said, finally closing his mouth. "What's going on?"

"Where were you headed, fellows?" Kit asked them.

"We were going to play the heroes, Montgomery," Kelly said. "I figured that we'd either steal Miss Shaw back from Puma or I'd end her misery. How'd you get out of this with a whole hide?"

Kit moved his injured shoulder a little and grinned. "Iron Claw wants justice for the murder of his sister, but he also wants peace. We are going in to discuss it with the captain."

Kelly sat tall in the saddle and looked at Iron Claw. "I was one of them, Chief. I shot the old man."

"Soldier Kit has told me this thing. He say you drink crazy water and then kill my people."

"That's right, Chief—but that's no excuse. I'm willing to take my punishment. If you've a mind to kill me here and now, I'll not put up a fight."

Iron Claw looked long and hard at Kelly. Then, looking very tired, he turned to Kit. "You told me of this man, Soldier Kit. I believe now that you told the truth."

"Al Squash isn't the same kind of man," Kit replied. "He is the one who started shooting your people. He is the one who caused all the deaths. I want him to stand trial."

"I'll help you round him up," Kelly volunteered. "That scum has caused me nothing but trouble. I intend to see that he faces up to the crimes we committed."

Kit looked over at Jeff. "You decided to ride along?"

"It seemed the least I could do. Kelly told me that he would need someone to take the lady to safety. Our ranch is still on good terms with the Owatawna. I figured I'd take her home with me."

Kit didn't like the sound of that, but there might be more trouble at the fort. He didn't want Deana to get hurt.

"I think that's a good idea, Deana," he said, turning to look at her. "You'd be safe until this thing is over."

Deana glanced at Jeff without expression. Kit had no idea what she was feeling or thinking.

"If that's what you want, Kit," she said finally.

It sure wasn't what he wanted, but it made sense. Farley's ranch was nearby, while the fort was at least a two days' ride away. Still, giving her to Jeff felt terrible.

"I'll ride back to Farley's place, once this is settled."

Deana lowered her eyes. "All right, Kit," she said very softly.

"I'll take good care of her." Jeff was suddenly all smiles and cheerfulness. "You can count on me, Montgomery."

"Yeah, I'm sure of that," Kit said sourly.

Deana looked up as Jeff started to lead the way down the trail. She opened her mouth as if to speak, then let the words die in her throat. Without so much as a wave, she followed Jeff.

Kit felt his heart sink. He should have said something to make her smile. He could have told her that everything would be all right. But somehow the words wouldn't come.

"Let's get going." Kelly didn't seem to notice Kit's inner agony.

"All right," Kit replied. "I'm looking forward to catching up with Al Squash. I hope he puts up a fight."

Kelly looked at Kit oddly. "You're in love with that little gal, aren't you?"

It wasn't really a question, so he didn't have to answer.

Kelly grunted in satisfaction. "I thought so."

"Who asked for your opinions?" Kit snapped.

"That was real neighborly of you to give your girl to Jeff Farley. He's been wife hunting as of late."

"She's got a mind of her own. She can decide what she wants."

"That's true enough, Montgomery. But you should have let her know there's a choice. I didn't see you try to kiss her."

"Knock it off, Kelly."

"All I'm saying is, you should have made certain the girl knew you loved her. Handing her over to Jeff might make her think she don't have a hold on you. It will be real awkward if he proposes to her before you get around to making that visit."

"Kelly, I'm warning you."

Kelly laughed. Then he smiled at Kit. "You know, I haven't laughed since this whole thing started. Even if they hang me for killing those Owatawna, I'll still thank you for straightening me out."

"One more crack about me and Deana, and

I'll hang you right here and straighten you out permanently."

They continued in silence. Kit couldn't help worrying that Kelly was right. He knew he should have said something to Deana. But he didn't know what to say. Did a man really have to tell a woman that he loved her? Couldn't she see it in his actions?

Kit had done everything he could to help Deana. He had risked his life for her more than once. He had fought Puma for her. But now he had to make sure there would be no war. Surely Deana knew that peace between the Owatawna and the Army was important for the entire country. She would understand . . . wouldn't she?

Chapter Sixteen

J eff put an arm around Deana's shoulders, but she deftly moved out of reach. He wasn't offended. He stepped up beside her and looked out in the same direction.

"Are you expecting Kit to return for you or something?"

"Something," she said, carefully evasive.

"We arrived only last night. Kit and the Indians won't get to Fort Ryan till late tonight or early tomorrow morning."

"I . . . he'll come out here, once the peace is secure. I haven't had a chance to speak to him. I—I owe him a great deal."

"Montgomery isn't the kind of guy to require eternal gratitude, Deana. He won't expect you to marry him or anything."

"I know."

"Shucks, Kit Montgomery has been negotiating the release of hostages for the past three years. I don't think he's ever gone out of his way to see any of them again. It's a job to him, nothing more."

She flinched at those words. "He'll come," she said firmly. "I know he will at least stop to say good-bye."

"What then, Deana? Have you given any thought to your future?"

She didn't tell him so, but that was the reason she wished Kit to return. She had to find out if what she felt was love or only gratitude. And what did Kit feel?

"I'm thinking of starting work on my own house next spring, Deana," Jeff was saying. "I told you about what I had in mind."

"Yes, I remember."

Jeff cast a sidelong glance at her. "It'll be a fine house for a family. Part of the herd belongs to me, and there's room enough to grow out here. A woman could do a lot worse than to burn her brand the same as mine."

"You'll make some woman very happy, Jeff. I'm sure of that."

He frowned, taking hold of her shoulders. She turned toward him, but held herself firmly away from his embrace.

"Don't let on that you don't know what I'm trying to say, Deana. I'd like you to become my wife. I promise I'd be a good husband."

Deana could see the man's good points. He'd stood beside her and Kit, risked his life at the way station. He'd even come after her with Kelly. He deserved more than she wanted to give him.

"I don't wish to make a rash decision, Jeff. I hardly know you."

"You can take some time to think it over. You're free to make up your own mind."

She forced a smile. "Let me think about it, Jeff. So much has happened. I haven't had time to sort out my feelings yet."

He relaxed at her answer and smiled in return. "Sure, Deana. I ain't pushing you. I know you've got a lot to think over. I just wanted you to know my position."

"And I'm very flattered, Jeff," she said sincerely. "Whatever I choose, I'll always have the highest regard for you."

He was satisfied to let the matter drop. There were chores to do, so he went to help. Left alone, Deana felt both fearful and uncertain. She wondered what Kit was doing at that moment. Was he thinking of her? Or had he forgotten her completely? What if he never came back?

She hated being assailed by so many questions. There were no answers to the riddles, but her head was full of them. She would put off

Jeff as long as she could, but if Kit didn't return, she would have to give the man an answer. That would be extremely hard, given her uncertainty. She needed to be with Kit once more, to test her feelings for a man who'd never so much as tried to kiss her.

Iron Claw stood tall and proud. He hadn't come to surrender, but to negotiate for peace. Captain Yount was smart enough not to place him under arrest. He listened to what Kit had to say, then rose to confront the chief.

"There have been many people killed," he said slowly and carefully. "It is hard for me to tell the high command in Washington that there will be no retaliation for the attacks on our people."

"The fight can end, Captain, or it can begin on a larger scale," Kit pointed out. "Iron Claw wanted to get even for the killing of his sister and those other Owatawna. He struck back at the wagon train after the unwarranted attack on his people. From that time on, he has been attempting to get the men responsible."

"And that's me and Al Squash, Captain," Kelly put in. "The soldiers who died were protecting us. That was also the case at the way station. If it had been against the law to kill those Indians, we'd have been locked up and none of the fighting would have happened."

"Puma wanted the lone survivor of the wagon train for his wife," Kit continued. "He had the idea that marriage to a white woman would give him the power to defeat the white race. Much of the killing was done by him and his warriors."

"And now Puma is dead," Yount said, recalling Kit's account of events.

"That's right, Captain. The decision for war or peace is in your hands. If you arrest Iron Claw and Two Hands, the tribe will declare war on every white in the country. Before this is over, every Owatawna, Cheyenne, Kiowa, Arapaho, and Ute will be involved in a full-scale war."

"What are the terms of this peace?"

"Simple enough," Kelly replied. "Al Squash and I are to stand trial for inciting a war by killing those first six Owatawna."

Yount looked hard at Kelly. "You realize that you could go to prison for a good many years?"

"It would be my life in exchange for several hundred, should war break out," Kelly replied. "I ain't afraid of hard work."

"This man has a good heart," Iron Claw

said. "The one called Al Squash is responsible. We want him to be punished."

"That'll be a little difficult, Chief. Squash left here the same day the stage arrived. He hired a couple of worthless characters and pulled out. I don't know where he went."

Iron Claw looked at Kit. "Is this your justice?"

"I'll find him, Iron Claw. Give me a few days."

"We'll send out some patrols and try to round him up," Captain Yount offered. "He's probably gone to do more trapping."

"Little Bear country," Kelly replied. "I can find him."

"If the man is caught and punished, there will be peace. If he lives to kill Owatawna again, there will be no peace!"

With those words, Iron Claw and Two Hands left the room. Kelly and Kit waited with the captain. Once they were alone, the captain turned his attention to the two men.

"I'm sticking my neck out to prevent more bloodshed. I'm going to wire the War Department and inform them that our conflict has come to an end. That means that you two men have to bring in Al Squash. He's the key to ending the fighting."

"I know where he'll head," Kelly said confidently.

"That you are helping the Army will be in your favor at the hearing. I don't make any promises. You might still end up in a stockade."

"We're wasting time talking, Captain," Kelly said. "If I know Al, he'll be wearing out horseflesh getting lost in the Little Bear Mountains. If we want him, we'd best get moving."

"I'm commissioning both of you to act on behalf of the Army. Draw what supplies you'll need from the quartermaster. If you need men, take the ones you want."

"Thanks, Captain, but Montgomery and I can handle the likes of Squash."

Kit nodded his agreement. "We'll be back as soon as we can."

"Good luck."

The two men left the room and went outside. Kit found the chief and Two Hands waiting to speak to him and Kelly.

"Will there be peace, Soldier Kit?"

"Kelly and I are going after Squash, Iron Claw. We'll bring him in to face the charges against him. The captain wants no more fighting."

"Do you wish the aid of my trackers?"

"Thanks, but no. We can handle it ourselves."

Iron Claw mounted his horse. He raised a hand in friendship toward the two men.

"Luck, Soldier Kit and one called Kelly. Bring this man who killed my sister. Bring him for white man's justice. This thing I wish to see. Two Hands will remain here and await word."

"We'll do our best, Chief. You have our word on that."

Iron Claw rode out of the fort, while Two Hands walked away. Kelly waited until they were both out of earshot before he turned to Kit.

"You and I know that Al ain't about to come without a fight. What if we have to kill him?"

"That will be white man's justice, Kelly. But first we've got to catch up with him. Al has two days' head start. We could be in for a long hunt."

"Better not take too long," Kelly said with a wink. "Jeff will be courting your girl every minute you leave her waiting. I still think you'd have been smart to kiss her. A gal needs something to remember."

"Don't start that again. Go round us up some horses while I get the supplies."

Even as Kelly went across the compound, Kit was thinking the man was right. He should have found time to be alone with Deana. By the time he returned to the Farley ranch, she might be promised to Jeff.

A knot twisted inside Kit's stomach. He found himself hurrying his step, eager to get moving. Time was not on his side. Somehow he had to get Al Squash and turn him over to Captain Yount. Then he would make a beeline for the Farley ranch. He had no idea what he would say or do, but he had to see Deana before she committed herself to another man.

Chapter Seventeen

Days dragged into one week, then another. Kit and Kelly couldn't catch up with Al. The man was not taking chances. His trail was hard to follow and he was wasting no time. The Little Bear country was only a hundred miles from the fort, but it covered about a thousand square miles.

As they approached Little Bear Lake, they got their first real break. They found the remains of a campfire less than a day old. Al had obviously not bothered to cover his tracks.

"We've got him now," Kelly said with a grin. "He's no longer worried about anyone following him."

"Any idea where he's headed?"

"There are some streams up the next mountain range. We picked them over the last time we were up here. I think Al is planning to winter up here and let things die down."

"Still two men with him?"

"It appears so. I think I know the ones. We dealt with the Sloan brothers once before. They're weasels."

"Can we overtake them tonight?"

Kelly looked skyward. "I doubt it. From now on, we'll have to be careful that we're not spotted. Al doesn't think anyone is behind him, but that won't stop him from keeping watch. Trappers always have to be careful in Indian country."

Kit felt that this whole thing was taking too long. He should have gone by Farley's place and spoken to Deana about what he was doing—and how much he loved her. He should have told her that when Al was in custody and the threat of war was ended, he wanted her to be his wife. What if she turned to Jeff in his absence? Kit felt he'd have only himself to blame if that happened.

The trees were still in the afternoon sun. The temperature was in the high seventies. The smell of wildflowers was in the air. The lake was deep blue and beautiful. Even the birds, squirrels, and chipmunks were chattering happily. It should have been a tranquil setting, but Kit was immersed in his own gloom. For him, the sun wouldn't shine until he was with Deana again.

* * *

Howie returned from his trip to the post. He spoke to Jeff for a time, then went in to be with his wife. Deana was doing most of the housework and the cooking. She felt she had to earn her keep, and Sandra was due to have her baby any day.

Deana had been watching out the window. She busied herself with the dough, preparing to make bread and rolls. When Jeff entered the room, she forced a cheerfulness she didn't feel.

"I see Howie made it back. Any word about the Indian trouble?"

Jeff came over to stand close to her. She paused to look at him, waiting for his answer.

"There's a warrant out for Al Squash's arrest. Two Hands is at the fort—a sign of good faith by the Owatawna. I think the fighting is over."

"What about Kit? Is he at the fort too?"

Jeff tried to look sympathetic. "Kit left the country. He stayed at the fort only one night."

Deana hid her pain as well as she could. "He . . . left?"

"Didn't even say good-bye to Sergeant Roaker. Howie spoke to him at the fort." Jeff hesitated briefly. "I don't think Montgomery is coming back."

Deana felt her heart sink. She turned to

shaping the bread, pretending to be absorbed in her work.

"You don't owe him anything, Deana. What he did for you, he would have done for anyone. That was his job."

She didn't reply, continuing to shape the dough.

"I'd like to marry you, Deana," Jeff said softly. "I'd like to have the wedding right away."

She stopped her work. "I told you, Jeff. I . . . I need time to think, to sort out my feelings."

"You can't pine over that wandering Indian fighter forever, Deana. He's left the country! He isn't coming back for you!"

"You don't know that for certain!" she retorted.

"He didn't send word to you. He didn't even come by the house and tell you good-bye. You were only another hostage to him, the same as all the others he rescued."

Deana shook her head. "I don't believe that."

"You love him, don't you?" he challenged her openly. "You're in love with him!"

"Stop it, Jeff. I don't want to discuss it."

"I want you for my wife, Deana. I want to marry you. Why don't we discuss that?"

She faltered. "I—I don't know, Jeff. I need more time."

"How much more time, Deana? How long do I have to wait?"

Squirming under his demand for an answer, Deana felt lost. What life would she have if she refused Jeff and ended up out on her own? He was offering her a home and a secure future. Unless Kit returned and gave her a choice, she felt that she had no options.

"Just a little longer, Jeff. Please."

He relaxed, putting a hand on her shoulder. "I don't want to push you, Deana," he said patronizingly. "But I want to get my own life sorted out. I want to start building our house."

"I understand."

He patted her arm and left the room. Deana slumped over the table, filled with dread and uncertainty. If he continued to press her for an answer, what could she do? He wouldn't be put off forever.

"Kit," she murmured under her breath. "Kit, why did you desert me? Why didn't you at least say good-bye?"

The blast of several rifles echoed off the mountain walls. Kelly reeled in the saddle, and Kit felt something slam into his left shoulder.

He and Kelly both landed on the ground at the same time.

Working his handgun free, Kit spotted the three men racing from cover. Al and the Sloan brothers had caught them cold. They were hurrying in for the kill.

Kit struggled to turn himself and aligned his sights. He fired at the nearest man, knocking him over. The other two broke off the charge at once, ducking for cover.

Kelly was hit hard. He held one hand over his chest and used his other to get his own gun out. His breath was ragged and uneven.

"Looks like I won't . . . won't be standing trial after all, Montgomery."

"Hang on, Kelly. I'll get you out of this."

They were pinned down in high brush, while Squash and one of the Sloans had the high ground. At least one of the Sloan boys was down with a slug in him.

Kit risked a peek over the top of the grass and got his hat shot off for the trouble. He ducked back at once and searched for an escape route.

Kelly grimaced from the pain of his own wound. He knew he didn't have much time.

"There's one chance, Montgomery. If we wait too long, I'll be dead and you'll bleed to death. We've got to get them now, while I can still help."

"What's the plan?"

Kelly forced a grin at Kit. "Simple enough. I stand up and draw their fire. It should give you a clear shot at one or both of them."

"That's suicide, Kelly. We'll get out of this. No need to throw your life away."

"It ain't been much of a life," Kelly said. "I was never worth nothing to nobody. If I can help save your life, I'll have made a contribution." He coughed and spit up some blood. His face was ashen, and his breathing was very shallow.

Kit knew Kelly was dying. He cocked his gun and waited, knowing he would get only one chance. If he missed, it would be over for both of them.

"You're good company to die with, Kelly," he told the man. "Let's see what Squash is made of."

"Take care of . . . of that little lady," Kelly barely whispered.

Then the man somehow managed to get his feet under him. He stood up and fired at the trees. This was his ultimate sacrifice—giving his own life to save Kit's.

Waiting until the two men opened fire, Kit found the second Sloan brother and fired. He turned his gun toward Al as Kelly fell at his side. Squash came out from his cover, his gun blasting away.

Kit rose up to shoot back. He felt something burn along his ribs, but he held his position. He found Al in his sights and squeezed the trigger. Al staggered when the bullet hit him, but he continued to come at Kit. Both men went on pulling the triggers until they struck empty chambers. Then the world was strangely silent.

Kit felt light-headed. His shoulder was on fire, and warm blood soaked the inside of his shirt on the right side. His hat was gone, and he didn't have the strength to hold up his pistol.

Al had blood on the front of his shirt. He took an unsteady step and sank to his knees. Al and Kit were frozen in time, each wondering who would die first.

"I hate your guts, Montgomery," Al said, cursing Kit.

"It's bad enough having to die out here," Kit retorted. "But it's worse being downwind of a skunk like you."

"Why don't you drop dead, Montgomery?"

"Why don't you?" Kit rejoined.

Al looked down at the blood on his chest. His eyes rolled. "Maybe I will."

Kit watched the man pitch forward onto his

face. He found himself getting dizzy, going down first to his knees and then to all fours. He had to check the Sloan brothers, make sure there was not enough fight left in them to finish him off. He also needed to stop his own bleeding and then bury Kelly. And then. . . .

But the world began going black before his eyes. He felt grass against his face and knew he was lying on the ground. As his consciousness was fading he thought one last time about the woman he'd left behind: *I love you, Deana.*

Chapter Eighteen

The post chaplain stood before the Farley family and looked over the small group of people. Deana's knees were weak, and her heart was pounding. She felt as if she were doing something terribly wrong.

"We are gathered here together to join this man and this woman in holy matrimony," the chaplain said.

Deana scarcely heard or saw him, though she was standing before him. This was the end of her single life. She was sealing her fate, marrying Jeff Farley. They would have a house by the stream, they would have children and a home. She should have been filled with joy and happiness. Why did everything feel so wrong?

"And if any man knows just cause why this union should not take place, let him speak now or forever hold his peace."

A wild, irrational hope seized Deana, and

she glanced over her shoulder. If only Kit would suddenly appear to save her.

But there was no outcry, and no one broke down the door to get into the Farley house. The only sound was that of Sandra Farley's baby fussing. All other voices were silent.

"Jeffrey Andrew Farley, do you take this woman to be your lawfully wedded wife?"

"I do," he said with a broad smile.

"And Deana Faye Shaw, do you take this man to be your lawfully wedded husband?"

Deana swallowed, hardly able to speak. "I . . . I. . . ."

The door was suddenly thrown open. All eyes turned to see a band of Owatawna entering the room. Sandra screamed, and several of the men tried to find their weapons.

"White woman is mine!" Iron Claw announced. "I will not see her marry this man!"

Warriors filled the room, many holding lances or guns. The few men present were disarmed and shoved against the wall. Then Iron Claw took hold of Deana's wrist.

"You come!" he demanded.

Deana had no choice as Iron Claw almost dragged her from the room. Once he reached the porch, he tossed her up onto a horse. A warrior to either side of her, she was quickly hustled out of the yard. She thought she saw

Sergeant Roaker entering the Farley house, but she couldn't be certain.

"What are you doing, Iron Claw?" she cried.

"White woman will be silent," he commanded. "You remember the last time I take you captive."

She remembered all too well. Falling silent, she concentrated on riding the horse. They rode at a fast pace, covering the ground as if pursued by the Farley men and the soldiers. They kept going until it was dark, riding higher into the hills to the Indian encampment.

The fires were low in the camp, and almost everyone was asleep. Iron Claw led Deana over to a tepee and dismounted. He pulled her off her horse and pushed her to the lodge entrance.

"You go in there! If you fight, I will see you bound to the stake at my own lodge."

She didn't argue, but entered the dark tepee and closed the flap behind her. It took a moment for her eyes to adjust to the dark.

A pile of hides and blankets lay near a fire of glowing coals. She decided that there was nothing she could do but make the best of the situation. Jeff wouldn't be long in getting the Army to act.

She smoothed her wedding dress and moved over to the blankets. Then she caught her breath. Someone was lying among those covers!

Kit had been awakened by the arrival of the horses. He roused himself to full consciousness as he found Deana standing over him. He blinked several times, thinking he was dreaming.

"Deana?" he whispered huskily.

She dropped to his side and put her face close to his. He could see her more clearly now. Her eyes were filled with tears.

"Kit!" she cried. "Oh, Kit!"

He grimaced and moaned slightly when she buried her face against his chest. Before he could say anything, she rose and pulled the cover back to expose his bandaged shoulder and ribs.

"You've been hurt!" she cried.

"Al and his buddies ambushed us. If Iron Claw hadn't followed Kelly and me, I'd have died for sure."

"What about the others?"

"I'm the only one left. Iron Claw brought me back here. I don't know how long I've been recovering."

"Did you send Iron Claw after me?"

Kit frowned, then looked more closely at Deana. "You're not dressed for travel. In fact, that's a fine-looking gown."

She lowered her head, as if ashamed. "I was going to marry Jeff. Iron Claw broke up the ceremony and brought me here."

That hit Kit as hard as either of the bullets that had wounded him.

"You were going to marry Jeff?"

She shook her head in frustration. "You didn't come back, Kit. Jeff kept after me. I had no way of knowing if you . . . if you even wanted me. I—I was. . . ."

"Then you don't love him?"

"No!" she said forcefully. "I love you, Kit! I've always loved you!"

He lifted his good arm and drew her down toward him.

Finally, between kisses, Deana asked, "What about Iron Claw kidnapping me?"

"If I know him, he got some help. Sergeant Roaker would be the kind to stage something as dramatic as kidnapping a bride."

"I thought I saw him enter the house."

"He and Two Hands got to be quite friendly. I recall Iron Claw saying something about that the other day."

"Then no one will come after us?"

"I'd say you're stuck with me. Jeff will have to find himself another woman."

"He'll make her very happy," Deana murmured. "Not as happy as the two of us, but very happy."

"If it's all right with you, I'd like to name our first boy after Kelly. He sacrificed himself so that I could defeat Al and the Sloans."

"I think Kelly is a nice name, Kit."

Kit kissed her gently. "I love you, Deana."

She smiled down at him. "You'd better never forget it. I was one I-do away from being Mrs. Jeff Farley."

"You save that I-do for me. I'll be up and around in another couple of days. We'll round up Roaker as best man and start making up for lost time."

Deana leaned down and kissed him again. "That sounds positively wonderful," she murmured.